Book of Ze'ev: 3

Sheyd of Gray

by John Baltisberger

An Aggadah Try It Publication

This one goes out to Max Bauman, Maxwell Ian Gold, and Josh Schlossberg.

My fellow Jews of Horror.

Chapter 1

Life had a way of dealing me a shit hand. I looked over the cards I held and sighed. Just like life, Father Jerry Mankowitz had dealt me a terrible hand. We sat at a little table across from one another in a run-down cathedral. The church had been condemned and had fallen into a terrible state of disrepair. Glancing around the large room we were in, it was easy to forget we were in Houston and not some crumbling old European city. Catholics loved their old-world aesthetic. I wasn't a gambling man myself, but Father Jerry loved to make bets. It was the entire reason I was here tonight.

I looked across the table at him. He was older than I was, starting to go gray, with a bit of a paunch. But he was a hard man. He looked like he would be more at home in a forest, wearing plaid and chopping wood, than on a pulpit. But monster hunting doesn't usually make for soft people, and I had no doubt that behind that paunch was a slab of muscle. He was a pale guy, Polish by ancestry, but I was willing to bet his pallor was more from being nocturnal than any other factors. I wondered what he thought about me. I was in my 30s, lean without being too scrawny. I generally wore slacks, tennis shoes, a t-shirt, and a sports coat of some sort. Only the fringes of my tallit katan and kippah would give anyone the idea that I was religious and not just another Austin hipster. I scratched my short beard while I considered the cards, though I already knew they were terrible and I couldn't win the hand.

I had come to Houston to introduce my apprentice and student, Sandy Cohen and Anthony Pelzatto respectively, to Father Jerry. I wanted to let them see that while the life of a mystic was lonely, it wasn't bereft of peers. People you could talk to, people who you could count on. Most people didn't spend their days and nights hunting cultists and nightmares, most people didn't even think those things existed. But once you knew, you couldn't help but see them everywhere. It made things like friendships and relationships hard—but not impossible. Then after the kids had gone to the hotel to crash, Jerry had grinned big at me and invited me to come see an actual vampire. What he had described to me sounded a lot like an alukah, a sort of vampire but nothing like you would find in an Anne Rice book. Alukah were more feral, bestial things that were like humanoid leeches with two mouths that tore their prey apart. And thus the bet. Jerry was sure it was a classic vampire, and I was sure it was an alukah.

Either way, this cathedral was perfect. It was situated in the middle of the creature's hunting grounds. An alukah would probably make this ruin its nest, somewhere safe that it could hunt from, and it would hate the intrusion. Likewise, a vampire would despise two holy men invading its territory. So, no matter who was right, we should be in a good place to do some hunting.

"Isn't it a sin to cheat?" I asked, throwing the cards down.

Jerry chuckled and took the thrown cards and the ante, which amounted to a few pennies, and reshuffled the deck. "I never cheat, cheating takes the fun out of it. I don't bet to win or bet to gain, I do it because it is uncertain. There is a thrill to it."

"My life has enough thrills, Jerry. Enough thrills without throwing myself on the dinner plate of an alukah, actually." Truth be told, though, if it was an alukah, it was my job to deal with it. If it was a vampire, Jerry knew all about that. Hunters like us tended to divvy up not by territory but by creature. There were just too many different things in the world for us to hunt everything there was.

"Well good thing it isn't an alukah then," Jerry answered. "I thought it would be good for you to see what an actual vampire looks like; you never know when that knowledge will come in handy. You can't go in assuming you know everything all the time, Wolf."

I screwed my face up at the nickname. A few people called me that, Jerry, Joe-Jack, people who knew me from when I was a kid, or people who just had too much trouble with *Ze'ev*. "I don't assume anything, Jerry. I just know that this thing is a predator and feral, not some Eastern European nobleman trying to nosh. I go into most things as if I know nothing; usually, because it's true." I grinned at him.

Jerry shook his head and dealt out another hand of cards, sliding his ante of a few pennies into the center of the table. I followed suit and lifted my cards—better this time, at least a little playable.

Jerry spoke as he looked over his hand. "Speaking of wolves ... Sandy mentioned you fought some kind of wolfman?"

"Yeah ... kind of. I don't know if he was actually a werewolf or just called himself that. But a guy named Peter Stübbe ... seemed to be around for a few centuries, lots of terrible shit. Was killing children." I didn't want to talk about the child-murderer; it was a dark place. And while all the bruises had healed, I didn't think I could ever forget the images from the crime scene photos.

"How did you stop him?" Jerry asked. His voice was soft, he knew this was delicate; but as a hunter and a holy man, he wanted to know how to stop evil in any situation.

"I beat him to death with a blessed baseball bat, and then I cut off his head, stuffed it with garlic, and buried his heart, body, and head in different locations near the crossroads." I met Jerry's eyes, watching them widen.

"That's a bit much. Did you really need to do all that?"

"I don't know, Jerry, but he could have been a werewolf, or a demon or just a sorcerer. I had no way of knowing what I was dealing with, and I figured it was better safer than sorry when dealing with a thing that was hunting down children for fun."

"Sandy also said you got to her without a car, across the state?"

"Sandy should maybe learn not to spill every trade secret," I grumbled. I knew what he was asking; he wanted to know if I had done something wrong, if I had dipped my toes into darker magic out of desperation. It was a common enough occurrence in our line of work, something we always had to be wary of. A good person damned by trying to use evil to their advantage. I didn't want to admit it to Jerry, but that was exactly what I had done. "There are some ways for the masters to travel quickly. It isn't pleasant, but by traveling through … "

I trailed off because Jerry's eyes had gone wide as he stared over my shoulder. I turned quickly in the chair and scanned the dim shadows, trying to spot what he had seen. "What?" I asked.

"I saw a man, just real quick-like, standing in the door looking at us."

"Your vampire?"

"No … not a vampire. Could be your alukah?"

"Nah, you would know if it was our alukah. Must have been your imagination." I looked back at my cards … and frowned.

A translucent goo had dripped from somewhere high above us onto the cards in my hand. You see it in horror movies sometimes. And then the person stupidly looks up in wonder, trying to figure out where it's coming from. Well, it isn't just bad writing, it's instinct. I craned my neck up to peer into the darkness of the steeple above. It took me a moment, but finally I spotted it, something large crawling across the ceiling. I toppled back in my chair, startled and not wanting to be directly under it.

Following my look, Jerry cursed and fell back from the card table as well, grabbing a long wooden stake from where he had placed it next to his chair. The thing fell from the ceiling, twisting and turning in the air before landing with a crash onto the table. The little table collapsed under the weight of the thing, and it scrambled to its feet. The thing turned out to be a young woman, well, mostly. She was white as paper, with wild, insane red eyes. Dressed in rags that barely hid her lean hard body, she looked like a homeless teenager who had spent every cent she was ever handed on a gym membership. Her blond hair was a tangled, matted mass, unkempt and unwashed. She had two extra sets of arms, eight limbs all told, and each of her hands ended in clawed fingers that dripped with gore, but that wasn't nearly as upsetting as her face.

Her face looked like someone had stretched a latex mask of a woman's face over a massive spider. Alien eyes peeked through torn flesh, the cheeks were torn open in terrifying mandibles that clicked and clacked as the girl-thing looked at me. Her nose was split open, revealing gray quivering flesh beneath it, but a long ivory proboscis jutted from the torn flesh, reminding me of a mosquito's mouth parts under a microscope. The translucent goo dripped from her ruined mouth, running over her broken teeth and twitching mandibles.

"What the hell?" I gasped, reaching for my gun. Before I could pull the weapon out, the thing took a swipe at me, knocking me back with deceptive strength hidden in those thin arms. I started to rise but chose instead to roll forward as the girl threw herself at me, silent but for the sound of her movements and clicking of her mandibles. No bloody screams or screeches, just a predator seeking to tear into prey. Jerry was trying to position himself behind the creature. I continued to roll and dodge the girl's attacks; she was quick and unrelenting. Finally, though, I was able to grab my butterfly knife from my coat pocket and flip it open.

The light off the silver blade caused the thing to pause. It paced back and forth, watching me from its too many eyes, trying to figure out a good angle of attack. I didn't want to give it a good angle of attack, not until I had a better angle of counterattack. But I didn't know anything about it.

"Jerry, what the fuck is this thing?" I asked, trying to

shift with it so my blade was always between us.

"Dunno, Wolf, maybe it's one of those alukah you keep mentioning," Jerry said as he approached it from behind, jumping back when it swatted towards him. Clearly, it had some of those extra eyes in the back of its head.

"You g-ddamn know it isn't."

"Don't take the lord's name in vain," he chided.

"G-d is a word, not the name for the creator," I argued back. Even facing down Spider-Man's pissed off sister, we couldn't help but banter.

"It doesn't matter if it's a proper name or not, it still has the, what do you call it, kavanagh, the intention behind it," he explained as he lifted one of the little folding chairs we had been sitting on and threw it at the monster.

It ducked under the projectile, forcing me to dodge to the side to avoid getting WrestleMania-ed. I spared a moment to glare at Jerry, but then the bitch was on me. I tucked my arms in close and adopted a boxer's stance, using my shoulders and forearms to block the brunt of the attacks. She was strong, the lean muscle wasn't just for show. I weaved under one set of arms and took a smack that staggered me back a few feet. The problem with fighting a woman with six arms was that she didn't leave a lot of openings.

But I could make some space. I flipped the knife in my grip and then threw it at the creature. The knife tumbled end over end before sticking into the thing's shoulder. I didn't take time to appreciate my throw—it's harder to land a knife throw than you might think. I was already reaching up to free my sidearm from the holster under my armpit. But the crazed woman was already on me again, still silent as she tackled me into a rotting pew. The wood gave way beneath us, and we tumbled onto the floor. I kept one arm close to my body, blocking the blows she was trying to rain down on my body, while I jammed my other elbow under its chin, just under the mandibles, trying to keep the snapping jaws and jabbing proboscis away from my face. Now that she was on me, it seemed she was intent on taking a bite out of me.

"Jerry! For fuck's sake! Would you do something!" I like to think I belted it out with some authority, but more than likely, it came out a little bit more of a panicked screech.

I saw Jerry over the shoulder of the creature. I don't know what he was thinking, but it looked like he wanted to make another quip. Instead, he lifted the stake high in the air and brought it down. The monstrous creature was so focused on me, it didn't even notice Jerry attacking it until it was too late.

The girl-thing threw her head back and let out a high-pitched whine of stale, blood-flecked wind before collapsing on me. It twitched and flailed. I was about to push it off me when it began unraveling, turning to ash against me. I watched its face as it withered away to dust and then crumbled to nothing on top of me. As soon as it was actually dead, I scrambled up and started brushing the remnants of the thing off of me.

"What the hell! They actually turn to ash?" I asked. I had never seen anything like that; all the monsters I killed left a corpse I then had to deal with. The Catholics had it easy.

"Yup, makes it real easy to not leave much of a trace." He sighed, looking down at the mess. "You okay?"

"Yeah, I'm fine." I pushed past him—maybe a little rougher than I had to, he did tease me before helping, after all—and pulled a cooler from behind a pew. Cracking it open, I pulled out two Shiners and offered him one. He took it with a look of appreciation.

"Nothing like a post-hunt beer." He reached into his jean pocket and pulled out a bottle opener, taking care of his and then mine before putting it back.

"Hear! Hear!" I agreed, clinking my bottle against his before taking a sip. "So that was a vampire ... not much like the ones in the media, are they?"

"Eh, some get it more right than others. But yeah, that's a vamp, a dead body possessed by a demon we call Beazzlebull."

"Just the one?" I asked, surprised by that. I always had visions of castles and nests filled with the things.

"Just the one as far as we can tell. Because the body is dead, exorcisms don't work. Stakes made of ash displace the demon, and it goes off to search for a new host."

"Still, just one vampire in all the world?" I was

having trouble with the concept.

"What? No, no, think of the vampires as puppets, or a colony with one brain, they're gestalt, or legion or whatever." Jerry grinned, he had been into biology before the call of the cloth and monsters had changed the course of his life. "They're all connected, but they suffer for it. The problem is it spreads the demon's power and intelligence out too, so the more vampires there are, the weaker each one is; the fewer …"

"The more powerful and dangerous," I finished for him.

He nodded. "So it's a balancing act. Gotta always keep one in our sights. It starts to get weaker, we know there are new vampires popping up; it starts to get too strong, we know we have a real problem." He shrugged and then paused, once again looking towards the entrance.

I followed his gaze and now saw the tall, gangly shape of a pale man in a suit.

"Weird, that isn't a vampire. Maybe one of your alukah? A demon, maybe?"

"No," I answered, putting down my beer and drawing my Jericho hand gun. I could see the power of creation and chaos coming off the man in distortion, like a heat mirage off a Texas highway during the summer. As dangerous as that vampiric creature had been, it looked like things were about to get a lot deadlier "No, that's a Sheyd."

Chapter 2

"Not everything is a Sheyd, Wolf," Father Jerry whispered, looking around for a weapon.

"Not everything, but some things are, and that is a Sheyd," I growled back.

"Some things are, but you think everything is because of the Sheyds."

"Sheydim," I corrected. "Plural is Sheydim. And I don't blame everything on them. But that? There? That man is a Sheyd."

As we argued, the creature stepped forward and began approaching us. At least that caused Jerry stop harassing me and focus on the threat.

We stood there; I had my gun pulled and aimed at the Sheyd at the far end of the church, Father Jerry brandished a sharpened ash stake awkwardly. That was the problem with specialists like him, they tended to forget protection from things they weren't hunting at any given time. I tried not to roll my eyes, important to present a united front in front of the Sheyd.

As he walked forward, he lifted his hands open-palmed towards us, as if to show he was unarmed and not dangerous. But I knew that was some bullshit. The Sheydim, creatures of chaos, woven from the pure stuff of creation, were capable of summoning weapons, using magic, or just ripping apart a human with their bare hands. Of course, that didn't mean it was what he was here to do. I'd had non-violent interactions with Sheydim before. But I would have been dead a long time ago if I didn't err on the side of caution, especially when dealing with them.

The Sheydim were half born, creatures first given life during the days of creation. The story went that as G-d was creating the universe, they were halfway through creating a new race of humans when the sixth day ended, the sun set and started Shabbot. To show the sanctity of the seventh day, to show that even G-d kept the sabbath sacred, G-d ceased work, leaving the Sheydim half finished. They were like mankind in many ways, they had the same appetites, the same freewill and ability to forge their own path. But they were also like angels, capable of being invisible, intangible. They were shape changers and tricksters, they were faerie and demon and everything in between. I didn't know if they could reproduce or if the Sheydim were sterile. I also didn't know if all the various creatures of folklore were simply different forms of Sheydim, but I recognized the aura that surrounded this one, a shadow of chaos, half angelic, half man, and ever-shifting.

The Sheydim could appear as almost anything. This one reminded me of that old Internet meme: a distressingly tall man that seemed stretched taut in a dapper black suit with fish-belly-white skin, just like the vampire we had just dispatched. But instead of being a faceless horror, the Sheyd wore a human face, fine bone structure, almost beautiful if not for a certain stretched out alien quality to it. His hair, blond and shoulder length at least, was pulled back in a low ponytail that I could see just over his shoulder. His eyes, huge and pale gray, watched us, seeming unconcerned with the weapons we had pointed at him.

When he was about 15 feet away, I waved the gun a little, slipping the safety off. "I think that's good. I think we can probably talk from there, actually."

He stopped and nodded, not lowering his hands. Anyone watching this would assume I was robbing a man. But luckily, or perhaps unluckily, the Sheydim loved ruins, abandoned was their favorite sort of descriptor; we were alone.

Jerry edged closer to me.

"What do we do?" he asked, waving his stake in a vaguely threatening gesture as though it would have any effect at all on the capricious half-born.

"We could talk," the Sheyd suggested.

Jerry scoffed, but I nodded. I didn't lower my gun, though; I didn't trust the Sheyd enough to not be scared out of my wits.

"We could," I agreed. "Probably not a bad way to start things off. What's your name?"

"Isingway," he responded, freely giving us a name, to Jerry's visible surprise.

"Isingway," I repeated, making sure I was saying it correctly, more to be respectful than any occult importance. There's this huge body of mythology that a name is important, that a true name is something sacred that must be protected, that if a demon, Sheyd, or faerie were to have your name, then it would own your soul, that it could control you. Of course, the opposite was believed too, that by knowing something's true name you had control over it, that names were in and of themselves power.

As far as I knew, that wasn't entirely true, at least not true enough to matter to most people. Words have real power; the words of creation, when spoken by someone who understands the true pronunciation of the words and letters, could mold reality and alter the world in strange ways. Names didn't factor into it, but identity did. Knowing something's true identity, their intention and mindset, could give you absolute control over them when paired with the right magic. Of course, knowing that could also give you absolute control over them just through emotional manipulation. Both were abhorrent practices, neither was something I would ever practice.

Besides, identity is something fleeting, a mercurial

notion that can and does change from moment to moment, especially in humans; so knowing someone's name and true identity in one moment may not be true seconds later. We as living things were too embroiled in the ever-evolving fabric of the story of creation to ever be static.

"Well, Isingway," I began, "I assume you know who I am at least, my colleague here is—"

"No need to introduce me to him, Wolf."

I glanced over my shoulder at the priest. He was all fun and games when he knew what we were dealing with; now that the ball was in my court, he had become gruff and unfriendly. I wasn't entirely surprised. It was his dogma: anything that wasn't human or an angel was some sort of demonic hell spawn, a servant of Satan. It's why these little get-togethers weren't very common. They turned nasty quick. I didn't argue with Jerry, though. I didn't want him to leave, but I also didn't want him to get us killed.

"Okay, so me, you know me," I said, turning my eyes back to the Sheyd.

He nodded.

"We haven't met, but you have met my brother." His voice was a whispered shadow thing that crept out of his mouth and wrapped around me before dissipating in the stagnant air of the church.

I watched his gray eyes, trying to stretch my memory for any meeting or encounter I had with Sheydim that might appear similar to Isingway. Of course, it was a stupid idea, the Sheydim had no physical form that they were tied to, they could be, and often were, anything they wanted to be. "I've had a few encounters with a few Sheydim; you'll need to narrow it down a bit for me."

"More than you would like to admit to, I'm sure," Jerry grumbled.

"My brother was posing as a police officer. He was attempting to contact you when—"

"Your brother, the one who has the centipede baby thing in his eyes?"

Of course I knew who he was talking about now. That Sheyd had stalked me while I was dealing with the werewolf child-murderer, pulling me over, terrorizing me. Hell, he had even gotten involved when I was attacked by the werewolf in a Whole Foods parking lot over in Bee Caves. I let out a breath of air. I suspected that this was going to go one of two ways. Either this was about Sandy Cohen, whom the Sheydim had been following and stalking before she came to learn with me, or this was about my traipsing through their city, a trip that had earned me the attention of some powerful supernatural forces.

"Haven't seen him since the incident with Stübbe," I finally said.

"Yeah, neither have I," Isingway responded.

That didn't necessarily mean anything; after all, the Sheydim were immortal creatures, not seeing someone in a few months over the course of several thousand years shouldn't mean anything. But the way he said it, there was weight to it.

"All right, and I take it that is strange, that your brother is missing. But I can promise you I don't have anything to do with that. I haven't seen him since that day, and I haven't done anything to harm any of the Sheydim."

"Not even Baladan?" he asked.

I winced. He knew I had tried and nearly succeeded in killing off the little gross imp. If not for the intervention of a much more powerful force, I would have destroyed Baladan.

"Well, even that I didn't have much luck in. So, why are you coming to me? I can't help you with this."

"Not only can you help me with this, Ze'ev Moshe Kaplan, you *will* help me with this. You will help me because not only were you the last tangible lead I have to my brother's whereabouts but because you owe the Sheydim."

I could feel Jerry's eyes boring holes in the back of my head. Like I said, he didn't distinguish between the Sheydim and demons. As far as he was concerned, I might as well have sold my soul to the devil if I was making deals with non-human entities. Jerry was a bit like my old Rabbi friend Nathan in that regard.

"And just what do you owe them, Wolf?" Jerry asked.

I rolled my eyes, bringing a smile to Isingway's face. "I owe them the life of my friends. I had a choice on whether I could save their lives or let them die. And at least in my faith, Jerry? Saving a life is always the right call."

"Not when it means your damned soul, Wolf," Jerry countered.

I rolled my eyes again. Another sticking point, another place where we would never see eye to eye. To him, the action, no matter the intention, could damn; for me, the intention was everything.

I turned back around to face the Sheyd. "Not here. You want to play straight with me, we'll talk in public. *Without* the peanut gallery provided by Father-almost-let-a-vampire-eat-me-and-is-now-acting-all-judgey. For now, you let us clean up and go."

Isingway nodded and walked backwards, never turning his back to us. He reached the door and promptly vanished into the darkness beyond. As soon as he was gone, I heard Jerry let out a long breath and turned to face him.

We were an ornery bunch, prickly lone wolves who had developed thick hides of spines to keep away anyone who could hurt us, or who we could get hurt. Jerry had his congregation, but to my knowledge, he kept to himself, a loner. But was I? I had Rivkah, Sandy, Anthony, Sara, and a whole slew of other friends. Maybe I was the weirdo here, maybe I was less a lone wolf than I always pictured myself. Or, maybe I was just less of an asshole than Jerry. He was packing up his gear.

"Sounds like you got a date with the devil there,

Wolf."

"Sheydim aren't demons, or devils, they aren't evil."

"Oh? Then why are you always crawling out of your skin about them?" Jerry countered.

"Because they aren't us, they're different, they have a different morality, different laws. For all intent and purposes, they're alien creatures. Too old to really get a grip on," I explained. I was sure I had explained this before, or maybe I was thinking of how I had explained the Sheydim to Sandy.

"Different morality? Listen to yourself, Wolf. Different morality." He scoffed. "There is moral and there is amoral. Our books aren't that *different*. I've read the Old Testament a time or two."

"Yeah, your Old Testament isn't the same thing as my bible."

"They're the same fucking book, Wolf."

"No, they aren't. Assuming you know about Jewish law and Jewish belief because you read a heavily censored and edited version of our book that was cut and pasted to a shape that pleased some old Christian king doesn't really make that much sense. We don't just have the Torah either, we have the Talmud, the Mishnah, a whole slew of holy books and teachings. Pretending anything is black and white, especially when it comes to living creatures, is inane. But I suppose black and white is sort of the Church's whole gig."

Jerry paused and rubbed his face. "Okay." He turned to face me, and I thought he would punch me for a second. "Okay, I don't know much about Sheydim, maybe they aren't demons. But I think it sucks getting involved in non-human affairs. Especially getting involved to the point where you owe them a favor. The world was made for us, Wolf. For humankind. Don't forget that while you're traipsing about with some inhuman fop trying to get him to a family reunion, that's all I ask. Just … stay human and stay human focused. Too many monsters out here for me to take them all on by myself." He offered his hand, a gesture of goodwill, an olive branch so that we didn't leave on bad terms, even if we were both still pissed off.

After a moment, I took his hand and shook it. "I'll always be here to protect people, Jerry. Nathan won't let me die or retire, so … you're stuck with me." I offered him a lop-sided smile and let him go.

He nodded his acceptance of what amounted to my own olive branch and turned away from me, heading out. He had driven us both here, but I think we both understood that we needed space to breathe. And besides, he was right, I had a date with a tall, dark, inhumanly handsome man.

Chapter 3

I caught a cab to the motel first, made sure that the kids were asleep. I cracked the door and saw the two lumps in the beds, Sandy's dirty blond hair sprawled around her pillow, and even in the darkness, Anthony's pale skin and white hair was almost luminescent. Sandy Cohen had come assigned to me by the Beit Din, the organization I worked for that helped maintain the safety of the Jewish people from supernatural threats. She had been a victim of a possession, and now because of that interaction, more creatures were taking notice of her. You could go your whole life without noticing anything supernatural, but as soon as you did, you couldn't stop noticing them, and they started noticing you too. She had only been my student for a few short months, but she had already been kidnapped by a werewolf, seen two exorcisms, and watched me nearly blow myself up with alchemy. She probably didn't have that much faith left in me. But she was a fifteen-year-old, scrappy as fuck, and was braver and more open minded than half the hunters I had met in my life. I just didn't want her to have to live the sort of life I eked out.

Anthony Pelzatto was different, and not only because he wasn't Jewish. Anthony had helped me catch up with and ultimately put a stop to a cult of necromancers led by a madman named Basken. Anthony was an orphan and had been punted around the system. Even at only seventeen, he had seen the worst humanity had on offer. He had pale white skin, shockingly bone-white hair, and fine features. He was gentle and meek as Sandy was rough and tumble. But Anthony was also different in other ways. He could see beyond the veil of reality into other worlds, cursing him with visions that the unnatural and inhuman of the world would love to make use of. I wasn't entirely sure of Anthony's human nature myself, but I had promised him I would help him figure things out, and since I was already playing school teacher to one precocious teen, might as well make it two.

The fourth member of my little team was back in Austin. Rivkah, my actual honest to G-d apprentice, was safe and sound at her home. When Sandy had been kidnapped, Rivkah had been hurt badly. I had called an ambulance but had then summoned a powerful Sheyd so that I could pursue the kidnapper and save Sandy. Luckily, Rivkah had pulled through all right and had forgiven me. Even if I couldn't forgive myself. Rivkah was important to me, and she deserved a friend who would put her first. But as with everything else in my life, chasing down evil had to come before everyone and everything else. My friendships, my physical and mental health, my romantic life …

I stepped back into the hallway and shut the door to the room as quietly as I could. I checked my phone for any missed calls or texts from my girlfriend, Sara. Nothing. That wasn't a great sign. She had been more distant lately, which was probably one reason I was checking at all, honestly; after all, it was close to two in the morning. I shoved my phone back in my pocket and shook my head. I was tired, exhausted, really. Usually when I stayed up all night and fought a terrifying monster from beyond the human realm of understanding, I would get to take a damned nap at least. That wasn't true. Life loved throwing punch after punch at me. Honestly, I was surprised Sara hadn't texted some passive, or maybe not so passive, aggression my way. But I could worry about that later. For now, I had to deal with Isingway.

The truth was that Jerry wasn't entirely wrong; I shouldn't be getting mixed up in the affairs of Sheydim. They were dangerous creatures, and their politics and political games spanned centuries. They were heavyweights in the mystical department. Last time I had tried to tangle with one of the Sheydim, I had almost been unmade by Lillith, Queen of the Demons, herself. But I felt like I was already in too deep. I had summoned one of their kind to take me from Austin to the outer edge of Texas to hunt down Peter Stübbe. I had put myself in this situation using treif magic. Now I had to pay the price and hope that it wouldn't cost me my life.

I used the elevator to go back down to the lobby, resting my head against the mirrored wall as it moved. Every fiber of my being was telling me to blow off Isingway and go to sleep. Sheydim, ghouls, vampires—I needed a break. Whatever happened to the days I spent my time breaking evil eye hexes and exorcising stubborn dybbuk? I stepped out of the elevator and saw the Sheyd sitting in the hotel lobby waiting for me. I rolled my eyes; he looked human enough that most people wouldn't give him a second glance. Well, they would, he was tall and pretty. People would stare, but they would be wondering who he was and if he was single, not worrying that he was an immortal creature of shadow and death. I nodded my head towards the door and walked that way myself. He could follow, but I wasn't about to hang out in a hotel lobby at two in the morning with him without a cup of strong coffee in my system.

I continued to walk, knowing he would follow. Just down the street a ways was a 24-hour diner called Ruth's. That would do. I pushed open the door and stalked in. I got a few looks, my kippah and tallit katan always got a few curious looks. Being an obvious Jew in the Lone Star State invited harassment. But I had grown used to it over the long years and could easily ignore it. Besides, most eyes turned away from me as Isingway entered. They had a new thing to stare at. I slid into a booth and looked at him. I was worried that he might be the sort to drink in the attention, but to my relief, he ducked his head and slid into the booth seat opposite me.

He started to say something, but I held up my hand, interrupting him. "Coffee first, then dire missions of life or death with monsters."

Isingway continued to stare at me, and I at him, while we waited for the waitress to come over. As soon as she did, Isingway's whole demeanor changed from inhuman creature of shadows to a disarmingly polite older gentleman. Even his features shifted, not so drastically as to be alarming, but I saw wrinkles deepen, crow's feet, thin lines from smiling and laughing, appeared as if they had always been there. "Hello, yes, sorry. Late night, isn't it? I think I will have … Oh, I would love a good waffle, and to drink, tea for me. I'm not as strong of stomach as my friend here."

I stared at him, wishing he would drop the act, it was almost too much. Almost. I saw the waitress, probably a college kid who had to choose between working in the diner and stripping, brighten at his kind politeness. She probably saw too many handsy, cruel drunks in here at these hours. She glanced at me, taking in my kippah and tallit katan before smiling.

"Shalom, mister. We got kosher biscuits and gravy,

if you want …?" Her accent was definitely Texan, but I recognized the northern coloration of a local kid raised by a New York Jew. I was just surprised to find it here.

"You have kosher biscuits and gravy?" I repeated. "Yeah, okay, sure; that and some coffee."

"You got it; the secret menu special and a waffle, tea and coffee. If you need anything, my name's Esther, just shout." She walked away.

I followed her with my eyes, suspicious of the coincidence. But the most sinister thing she did was put our order in and then sit with a group of other waitresses that looked like they could all be siblings. I turned my eyes back to Isingway.

"Can I speak, or do I actually need to wait for your coffee?" he asked, and then nodded when I waved him on. "I know my brother was looking into you. You had been poking around in places that humans generally don't, and, well, as both a Sheyd and a cop, he wanted to know what you were up to."

I met Isingway's eyes and then turned to watch the slow foot traffic of drunks leaving their favorite haunts to trudge back to whatever half-life they called their own. I wondered if Isingway saw any humor in that, the way the humans lived these half-lives willingly and in such a brief span while the Sheydim were condemned to half-lives for eternity. Probably not; it's probably one reason so many of the Sheydim were angry with humankind.

"So, your brother, what was his name? I only knew

him as Officer Stevens."

"Oronymous. I called him Oro. I think he went by Oscar in his human life."

"Oro," I repeated. I pictured the hollow-eyed Sheyd in front of me. He had bled malice, but on the other hand, he had probably saved my life when I confronted him in the parking lot of the Whole Foods. If not for him, I probably would have been killed by Stübbe and his wolf. "Oro was posing as a human, and as a cop … why? Why was he posing as a cop?"

"Well, he wasn't posing as a cop. He went to the academy, he graduated, he pulled a salary, he was a policeman," Isingway said, looking irritated.

"But why? Why would he do any of that? He didn't need money; as far as I know, your kind don't even need to eat." I leaned back as the waitress, Esther, brought by the plates and poured our drinks. As soon as she stepped away, I dug into the biscuits. They were delicious. Ridiculously so. It was rare that you could eat something as good as real southern biscuits and gravy and keep kosher at the same time. I pointed my fork at the Sheyd as I swallowed.

"So why was he doing all of this? If I'm going to help you, it would help to know more about the whys."

Isingway shrugged a little, cutting into his waffle, spreading the butter and syrup around in lazy spirals. "I can't tell you everything, I just … I can't. But I know what you're really asking. Was this part of some great scheme to control and hurt humans, was this diabolic?

And no. No, it wasn't, Ze'ev. My brother loved your kind. He enjoyed how much passion and life you pack into such a short amount of time; he was nearly a zealot about protecting you all. Not everyone has their own personal monster hunter on call, and through his work as a policeman, he was able to track and stop threats that weren't on your radar. I promise, while he may not have been perfect and he may have terrified you, he was a good Sheyd, and a well-meaning one."

I took in all of this. Oro had been terrifying, an empty eye-socket man with sharp features and a baby-faced centipede crawling around in his skull. Maybe the man shape was Oro or maybe the centipede thing was, I didn't know. What I did know was that Isingway seemed to be honest. Of course, all of this could be an act, it could all just be a trap to lure me into a vulnerable position and kill me on behalf of Baladan or any number of nasty things I had crossed wrongways during my time on this earth.

I took another bite of biscuit and nodded. "All right, so, fine, he was just a cop and my poking my nose into some pretty bad things caught his attention. It is my job to poke my nose into bad things, to be fair."

Isingway didn't look convinced. Which was also fair.

"Look, I have to get my students back to Austin tomorrow, but after that, I can come and we can figure out a starting place for all of this."

"That's fine. I'll head to Austin as well; it is as good a place to start as any, seeing as that is where he was when he disappeared." Isingway stood, leaving his waffle unfinished, practically untouched, and headed for the door. I watched him leave. I needed to get back to my room and get some rest too, but I would be damned if I was going to let those biscuits go to waste. As I ate, Esther came by.

"Your friend didn't like his food?" she asked.

"I think he just ordered to be polite; not that polite, he left me with the bill. But these are great."

"Thanks. Momma learned to make them when she moved here, wanted to keep Daddy happy. You need anything else?"

I shook my head and smiled, the sort of smile southern Jews give each other when they're pleased to find another Jewish person in the wild. "No thanks," I finally said after I had finished my last bite and handed her a small wad of bills to pay for everything, including the untouched food. "Tell your mother thank you, and I'll definitely be back next time I'm in town."

I stood, gave her a small wave, and left the diner. I had a big day ahead of me, and I needed to get at least *some* rest.

The car ride back to Austin was not a quiet one. The kids had complained about getting up too early, even though both of them had been dropped off at the hotel around ten. I assumed they had stayed up texting and

TikToking or whatever until at least midnight. I was the one who had to fight a damned vampire and then have midnight snacks with a Sheydim. We grabbed tacos on the way out of town as I filled my little car's tank. I knew how to get them off of their whining, I just wasn't sure it would be better.

"Father Jerry and I fought a vampire last night." As I predicted, both teens went silent, wordlessly putting their phones down. I smiled, glancing in the rearview at them both. "Just in case you were curious what we were up to."

"A vampire? Like Anne Rice?" Anthony asked.

I looked over at him, concerned that was the first vampire related content he could think of.

"Not like Twilight, I hope," Sandy chimed in. "Did you beat up Edward?"

Ugh. I made note to show both of them Gary Oldman's Dracula, or maybe Nosferatu, something that had a bit more teeth than Tom Cruise or Robert Pattinson.

"No, not like either of those," I answered, regretting that I had brought up vampires at all. "You know, almost every culture in the world has some legends about vampires or vampiric beings. Judaism is no different."

"Sort of like werewolves?" Sandy asked. She had firsthand experience with the same werewolf I had, so she had developed a bit of a fixation on them—a dangerous thing, though I suppose if someone was going to become a werewolf hunter, I would probably put my money on Sandy.

"Yeah, it's sort of exactly like how most cultures have werewolf legends. But while I don't know much about werewolves, I can tell you the thing I fought last night wasn't like any of the vampiric monsters I've fought in the past. According to Father Jerry, it was a demon."

That caught Anthony's attention. He was Catholic, anything that smacked of the church or of demons or anything like them made him perk up.

"I thought you said it was a vampire," Anthony objected.

"I did."

"I thought you said the Sheydim weren't evil."

"I ... sort of did," I corrected. "I said they aren't all evil, or all good, and besides, this isn't that sort of demon," I explained. "Sheydim are part of the natural order, created by HaShem; demons, or at least what I call demons, are something else. Think of them like the Nephilim."

"Half-Angels?" Anthony asked, his eyes bright with lust for knowledge.

"Eh, half angel, half Sheydim, half something else; they're creatures that aren't supposed to be, things that go against the natural order in more than just an organic or magical way. They are ..." I struggled to think of a good example. "Think of our reality like a lake. It connects by stream or river to other bodies of water. Sometimes animals from the river or even brackish water end up in the lake, no big deal. Those are supernatural entities, things that belong but may not be perfectly suited for our human world. Well, demons are like if a saltwater octopus mated with a crawdad. That isn't supposed to happen. The octopus shouldn't be here, it shouldn't be able to mate with the crawdad, and the resulting being is the demon."

I glanced in the mirror again. Both teens were staring at me, stupefied; my explanation meant less than nothing to them. "Just keep in mind that our language is limited and the word *demons* means a million things in a hundred different languages and across a thousand different cultures and times, okay?" I waited for them to both digest that.

"So, what was the vampire? You said it wasn't like stuff you have seen before?" Sandy finally asked.

"According to Jerry, all vampires, or at least all of this kind of vampire, are a single demonic entity that spreads itself through a lot of different bodies."

"So, it possesses them?" Sandy clarified.

"Yeah, possesses and changes them. I think the host body dies because of the mutations, so I don't know if an exorcism would work."

"So how did you guys stop it?" Anthony asked, rapt.

I met his eyes; they were so pale as to almost be white, like they had been made from silver. He was such a strange looking kid. He wasn't albino, but he looked like all the color had been drained from him. Part of the curse or blessing that turned him into some sort of empathic psychic. I wondered if he had seen something terrible, knew some truth that made him more fascinated with demonkind than was necessarily healthy. I turned my attention back to the road. Contemplating that had no healthy end for me.

"Father Jerry stabbed it in the heart with an ash-wood stake," I admitted.

"What?" Sandy cried in delight. "Like, literally a stake through the heart? Like in the movies? Oh my G-d, did it look like a movie vampire? Did it fly or turn into a bat?"

I waved off the barrage of questions from Sandy. "No, none of that. It looked like a spider wearing a human costume, and it was strong and fast. Stronger and faster than I would have liked it to be." I grinned. "Look, the fact is, it was a dangerous creature that was preying on humans in Houston. It wasn't a Jewish monster, it wasn't targeting Jews, but Father Jerry asked for my help and I gave it. You never have to go through all this shit alone. That's the lesson here; keep your friends closer than your enemies."

"Isn't the saying keep your friends close but your enemies closer?" Sandy asked skeptically.

"It is," I answered. "The idea being that's how you keep an eye on your enemies. But I find having a friend at my back to help keep an eye on said enemies is a lot more useful."

Speaking of the friend at my back, I wondered how Rivkah was doing. She had recently returned to working in the little warehouse workshop. She handled a lot of the scientific and alchemical research we did. She was brilliant, and bridging the divide between mysticism and science was her passion. It didn't have a lot of application; after all, I didn't need to know why the ash stake had killed the vampire, I just needed to know it would. But we as a people were always hungry for knowledge, for answers, and so the Beit Din continued to pay for her research and continued letting me utilize her services.

I flipped my music on, scrolling through my music until I found something that wouldn't make the kids moan, but also wouldn't give me a headache, to finish out our last two hours of driving back to Austin.

Chapter 4

I dropped Anthony off at his place, a small efficiency on the south side of town, before driving Sandy all the way up north to where she was staying with Rivkah. I didn't get out of the car and see her to the door or anything, I would see Rivkah tomorrow. And I knew once she knew I had seen an honest to G-d vampire, she would have a lot of questions. Questions that would probably then lead to me having to tell her about the damn Sheyd. And those were questions I really didn't want to get into just yet. I glanced at my phone, still nothing from Sara. I considered driving by her place, maybe surprising her. Bringing her dinner and flowers would do some good, help repair the damage my constant absence had caused.

It wasn't like I was gone because I didn't want to see her; I loved Sara, I loved being around her, her laugh, her kindness, her passion. Everything about her was beautiful and amazing. But I had spent months trying to take down a horrible cult of necromancers led by a madman named Basken, and I couldn't risk exposing her to that, and I certainly couldn't tell her the truth. No, despite how much I hated lying to Sara, to everyone in my life, the truth would get me locked up in a pen. Or worse, they would believe me and be targeted by all the things that go bump in the night that I tried to keep them safe from.

I decided not to stop by her house; she might be at work, or more likely, sleeping after an all-nighter at the hospital. Her grueling schedule as a nurse kept her busy and was probably one of the only reasons we were still together. She didn't have time to notice how often I was missing. I sighed, switching the music over to Pink Floyd's *Division Bell*, a great melancholy record to be bummed out to. Sometimes we just had to feed the great hole in ourselves that was filled with sadness. I made note to head to the synagogue tomorrow for afternoon meditation with Rabbi Folberg. It wouldn't help me with my current work load or figure out anything with Isingway, but it would help me recenter. It would help me reconnect to my community. Just like I had told the kids, you never had to be alone.

While almost everything I did was for the Jewish people, sometimes I felt separate from them, like I was an outsider. I felt like my faith was weaker but my belief was stronger. I'd met angels. I'd wrestled Sheydim and come face to face with dybbukim. But I didn't go to shul every Friday, let alone every Saturday. I didn't make it to Torah studies when I did go. I probably looked like a very half-ass Jew from the perspective of most people. Maybe I was. I said my prayers in the morning when I woke up and before I went to bed if I wasn't too tired. But sometimes I forgot that Judaism wasn't just a religion of belief or ritual. It's a faith of community.

Making the decision to go and be a part of a service made me feel lighter than I had felt in days. Maybe some restful, mindful meditation would help set my mind at ease and make my path forward with Isingway clearer. After all, dealing with the Sheydim was never straightforward. They were strange creatures, almost angelic in some ways but horrifying at the same time. I flipped the music off after a few moments and drove in silence.

What if it was a trap? The Sheydim were shape changers, capable of appearing as anything they wanted to. Maybe Isingway was Oro. Maybe I was being tormented by a single entity. But why? I considered all the possibilities I could come up with at that moment. If Isingway was the same Sheyd that has stopped me before and Oro was a fiction he created, he could be using me to get close to Sandy. Or maybe there was some truth to his lies and he wanted to know why I was poking my head around forbidden and terrible texts. Or maybe he was being honest.

Maybe Isingway was who he said he was and Oro was a good man—well, Sheyd—who had gone missing.

If it were me, I would certainly follow up with where he had last been investigating. Which was, again, me. That made my stomach settle coldly in my gut. I didn't like the idea that I was drawing that much attention to myself. And I wasn't even doing it for myself. I was gathering these damned books of black magic for Mr. Grin, the horrifying ghoul who wanted to kill off his lord and master, Baalrachius. After I had used the ghouls to take out Basken's cult and pulled a fast one over Grin, he had basically threatened my life and the life of everyone I cared for unless I did his chores. And so far, his chores consisted of finding darker books of magic that were hidden in Texas. I assumed he had other little gophers in other parts of the world to get the other books he might want. I hadn't figured out how to get out of it yet.

Ideally, I could kill Grin and end him as a threat to the world, but as far as I knew, he was the only thing keeping Baalrachius off my throat. If the King of Ghouls learned that I was still alive and Mr. Grin hadn't killed me, we would both be dead before sunrise the next day. I groaned to myself as I pulled off the highway. How did I get embroiled so deeply with the monsters I was supposed to be hunting?

I drove down Riverside and looked at all the new developments. Soon I wouldn't be able to live here. Back when I first moved over here, it had mostly been a lower income area, primarily Hispanic. Now the gentrification of the neighborhood was out of control. More rich white UT kids than anything else, hip restaurants with names like Mod and Chi'lantro. It wouldn't be long before I was priced out. I would need to find a new cheap place to crash. It wasn't that the Beit Din didn't pay me enough to survive and live in a decent place, but I was helping my sister pay my mom's rent, and since she moved back to New York, it wasn't cheap.

My apartment wasn't very big, just one of a dozen or so within the Landry Place apartment complex, but it was a pretty little area. It had a pool and a volleyball court, a small gym with a bunch of broken equipment, everything I needed to be a man living on his own. I circled the complex looking for parking before finding something in the shade—not too close to my door, but the shade was a precious commodity in Texas. I parked and got ready to get out when my phone started ringing. It was Nathan. My boss. I groaned; it was as if he could always tell when I was coming home from a long night. He must have a sensor in his house for when I'm exhausted and can't take anymore.

"Hello, Nathan," I answered.

"*Ze'ev, I'm glad you answered.*" He spoke in Hebrew, he always spoke in Hebrew. I think it made him feel holier. "*You're needed right away, South Austin, there's been an incident at the zoo.*"

I didn't know what to react to first: the fact that apparently Nathan out in New York had relevant information about something in Austin before I did or the fact that there was apparently a zoo in Austin. I decided not to question either at the moment.

"What? What happened?" I asked as I got out of the car and headed for my apartment.

"Demons, Ze'ev, demons happened, malikim, Ser'im, kesilim, demons."

That brought me up short. Demons? It was the middle of the day, and Nathan wouldn't make the mistake of conflating demons and Sheydim.

"Well, which one is it?" I asked. If there were demons running around in daylight, that meant something was seriously fucked and I needed to be prepared.

"I don't know. The ones who called this in don't know how to differentiate between these things!" Nathan snapped at me.

Perfect. Without knowing what I was up against, I had to sort of wing it, and there was no faster way to end up dead than just winging it. I went inside, not bothering to close the door as I sat at my computer and pulled up my browser to google Austin zoo.

"Ze'ev? Are you on your way?"

"I will be, but, uh, which zoo?" I finally asked.

I had to stop by the lab on my way out towards Bastrop. I hadn't brought anything with me for hunting monsters when I took the kids to Houston. Despite everything, I tried not to spend every minute of every day assuming I was about to be attacked. I grabbed a duffel and filled it with a few weapons, a few tricks that could be used to counter other things' magic, and a fistful of charms. You never knew what you would have to deal with in any given situation. I also kept my Jericho hand gun on me nearly all the time now. It wasn't that I loved carrying a hand gun, it was that life had taught me I could actually, and probably would, be attacked by a madman with a knife at any given moment.

Thus armed, I headed out towards the Capital of Texas Zoo to see what the hell was causing enough of a panic for someone to actually want to speak to Nathan. The parking lot was full of crying children and angry parents. I saw a school bus in one corner, where a teacher was desperately attempting to calm down their students. It looked like whatever had happened had really disrupted the goings on at this little zoo. I pushed my way past the grumbling parents that were gathered outside and walked towards an older woman carrying a clipboard; she looked like she was probably the one in charge.

"Sir, I'm sorry, but the zoo is currently closed," she said, raising a hand to stop me. She looked haggard. "We're working on addressing the issue as quickly as possible."

"Oh, actually, I'm here because the zoo is closed. I was called …"

She stared at me for a minute and leaned forward, trying to whisper above the sound of people shouting.

"You're the … the hunter?" she asked. I could tell she

felt stupid and ridiculous asking. She was in over her head.

"Something like that," I said, feeling equally ridiculous.

"Okay, go inside. Cathy and Mitchell will fill you in." She looked at my kippah, tallit, and duffel bag and shook her head, clearly mystified by my appearance. But I was used to that, even when I wasn't being called to a zoo to look for a demon.

I stepped into the main office in front of the zoo and saw a young woman, whom I assumed was Cathy, and an older man, who for all the world looked like he had stepped off the cover of an advertisement for a dude ranch. The cowboy looking man nodded his head at me and offered a hand. I shook it; it was warm and worn, but firm.

"Howdy. Ze'ev, right?"

"Eh, howdy," I returned the greeting. "Yeah, I'm Ze'ev. You must be Mitchell. You called Nathan?"

The man scratched his chin and shook his head. "Well, I called your momma, figured she would know how to get a hold of you." He laughed at my blank stare. "I knew you when you was growing up, Ze'ev. I was friends with your daddy. I remember, well I remembered, all that mess back then, remembered about what your momma said, sort of thought this might be in that wheel house."

"Huh. Nathan neglected to mention my mom," I admitted. "Uh, I'm sorry, Mitchell, I got to admit, I don't have a great memory for names and faces."

"Don't worry about it, Ze'ev. Like I said, I grew up with your daddy. You used to play with my kids, but it was a long time ago."

I nodded and glanced at the young woman. She was watching us, pale and trembling slightly. Whatever was going on had spooked her but didn't seem to bother Mitchell as much. But according to the old man, he had been around when things got bad back in Crisp.

"Okay, well, I'm here to help. What's going on?" I asked, angling my body to face both Cathy and Mitchell, hoping including her and letting her know I was going to do something would calm her down.

"Well, when we got here this morning, there were some animals that had been killed. I figured it was coyotes, or maybe even teens, you know? So I got started cleanin' up the mess, but Cathy here saw something and—"

"Monsters, I saw monsters, they're still out there!" she cried.

"Monsters, okay." I spoke as calmly as I could, hoping to reassure her. "What did the monsters look like?"

It didn't look like I was helping much; her blue eyes were wide with fear. She looked like she had been in the midst of a panic attack since she had spotted the creatures, whatever they were. Now she looked at me in horror, as if my question had just made her realize that there was more than one kind of monsters. The one positive here was that she was old enough that this probably wouldn't magnetize her to the world of the supernatural as it had with me and Sandy.

Mitchell waited a moment, giving Cathy a few moments before he turned and shrugged. "Uh, I thought they were mangy dogs or coyotes at first, actually. They got into the wolf enclosure and pretty much tore through the big dogs."

Wolves. I wasn't too keen on dealing with wolves. Not after what Sandy and I had gone through so recently. My thoughts were interrupted by the sound of a snarl, which caused Cathy to squeal and hide behind Mitchell. It definitely didn't sound like any coyote I had come across.

I glanced at the two and nodded. "Well, why don't you both wait here. I'll go check it out, let you know if I need anything ..." I walked away, leaving Mitchell to comfort Cathy while I dealt with G-d-knew-what.

I worked my way through the lines of enclosures. The zoo wasn't like the big zoos in San Antonio or Dallas, it was more like a large kennel for exotic animals. In the few minutes I had spent on the website, I had seen that all the animals here were rescues from people who had smuggled the animals to Texas. Most of them were being rehabilitated for release in the wild or socialized for use in education programs. Still, I wouldn't want to be stuck in an enclosure along a Bastrop back highway if I were one of these animals. The animals were subdued. Each enclosure I passed, I, noticed how the animals, primates and birds mostly, didn't even turn to look at me. They mostly hid silently in their hides or under their bedding. I was getting a little freaked out.

I finally rounded the corner and came face to face with the wolf enclosure. My stomach lurched. Inside were three … things. At first, I thought they were rotting ghouls. But they weren't ghouls. Ghouls, for all of their monstrosity, were mostly human looking. These could never be mistaken for humans. They had the same short snouts and brutal teeth as the ghouls did, but from there, the similarities were mostly superficial. Their hair was bristly and rough, growing in irregular patches all over their bodies. Their eyes, or eye sockets, were pools of darkness weeping inky black tears that seemed to swallow light. The rotting bestial things' limbs bent at unnatural angles, and as they moved in the fenced in area, it reminded me of a spider picking its way across uneven terrain. I could smell them from where I stood; it smelled like gasoline and spoiled fish. I knew what they were. I had never encountered one of the Ser'im before, but the encounters I had read of described the terrifying destruction of light in their gaze, and the odor.

I froze. I felt like I needed to get the drop on them, but these were literal demons. I didn't know what I could use to really enact their dispersal or destruction. There were plenty of charms and invocations, specific psalms that could be used. I had glazed over them plenty of times. But actual demons, that took preparation to deal with, prep I hadn't done yet. I took a step back, hoping to retreat and make a plan while they were tearing apart the poor wolves in the enclosure. Before I could, though, one looked up and saw me.

"Oh look. He come." The voice rumbled out like an earthquake, a deep rumble like two stone slates rubbing against each other. This one looked powerful, swollen with grotesque muscle, the promise of violence and rage thick in the air around it.

"He come?" a second asked, its voice high pitched and piercing. Unlike the first, it was gaunt, a stringy thing that looked like it was starving. It looked the most like a ghoul as it looked up, angling one of its void eyes in my direction. "He do, that he do! Thought we would tear through more animals first. He come too quick!"

The third, an obese creature that seemed to slide and flop about as it moved, picked up a wolf's decapitated head and jammed its tongue in the eye hole as if searching for more goodies inside. When it had finished, it tossed the head aside and sat back, regarding me with an amused grin on its horrifying face. "He is inconsiderate of hunger, inconsiderate when we have worked so diligently to make him feel comfortable." His voice was the most human, and probably the most terrifying for being so. While the other two seemed bestial and feral, this obese wart of a monster was thoughtful and well spoken.

"Considerate?" I asked when I thought I could speak without losing my proverbial lunch.

"Consider it," the deep-voiced thing said.

"He considers!" from the screeching one. A veritable Greek chorus of terrifying voices.

"Consider, that we come to this place, close to you, we come to this place where you faced the wolf, and we kill the wolves. Ah? It is kind, it is thoughtful, you should be thoughtful too. Mindful of the great lengths we go through to make this meeting happen, to extend an olive branch to the despoiler. He shouldn't read it as a threat of what we will do to other more human shaped wolves."

"Despoiler? Threat?" I was trying to follow, but the way the Ser'im echoed each other, creating a round out of their own statements, was filling my head with a terrible buzz.

"Ze'ev, wolf of Texas, this conversation will take too long should you only repeat after me what I have said." Each of them only stood about 4 feet tall, hunched over on all fours like felines. Their back legs looked powerful though atrophied, their front limbs were long, too long, and bent unnaturally as they tore ribbons of flesh off the still cooling bodies of wolves. "You despoiled the City East of Nod with human footsteps, human words, human breaths. It stinks of you there now."

"I was given safe passage through that place," I murmured. A cold lump had formed in my chest and was radiating out to my hands and feet. I had actually been given passage, but I had also promised not to hurt anyone there, and I had almost immediately gotten into a fight, a fight that was only ended when I had come face to face with the First Woman.

"Oh? And is he who gave passage here? Do you see the one who let you bring your human stink to our home here, with us, now?" All three Ser'im made a show of looking around the enclosure, making a point to pick up the bits of wolf they had strewn about the area to check under the mess they had created. "No … no … it seems we are alone."

I considered just pulling out my gun and shooting. I also considered which true pronunciations I might use, but the Ser'im, to my knowledge, had been created outside of reality, created by something other than HaShem, in a corner of unreality left unfinished. Would the words and letters of creation have any effect on them at all?

"Your death is ordained, it is ordered, it is requested." The fat one reached under the folds of its skin and brought out a shard of something. Like its eyes, it dripped with darkness, sucking in light and dimming the world around it. The object was painful to look at, not just because of the horrible way it devoured light, but I had the distinct feeling it was unnatural, completely treif, a polluted chunk of reality held in the hands of something that should have never been. It looked like a broken mirror that reflected only pain. "We bring our kelipot, our nogah, and they are fed by you, Ze'ev, and as it grows darker with your deeds, you come closer to the embrace of damned things. The woman of the statue sends her greetings and spills the blood of those she loves to see it done."

"You're assassins, sent by … a statue?" I stuttered, trying to decipher what the fuck the creature could be babbling about. I had pulled out my gun when the thing withdrew what it claimed was one of the kelipot. The kelipot were husks of darkness and sin that hid the divine light of creation, an active ingredient in keeping the world from healing. "Seems like a bit of overkill. Three Ser'im bearing kelipot for one mortal man."

"Overkill? Yes." All three things chittered and laughed. "But it is a contest, a contest between us. Who will claim your skin? The game is no fun if you are unaware, too easy to kill, too easy to strip down to components like these." It gestured to the remains of the wolves all around it. "So we warn, let us play cat and wolf."

"Cat and mouse," I corrected almost mechanically.

"No, you are wolf, we are the Ser'im, you look at your future." The creature tucked the shard of blackness back into its folds, offering me a hungry look. "To each their own, Ze'ev, to each their own, and to each our own as well. We take turns, we make bets, the killing of mortals is boring work and we must make it interesting somehow. Perhaps, you at last will be more interesting, more enticing than the last." It shrugged its shoulders, and the three things turned and began loping away on uneven limbs. I saw now that they had torn a hole in the fence of the enclosure on the far side of the zoo.

Small comfort that the things were somehow bound by something resembling time, space, and the laws of physics.

I stood there holding my breath until the three demons were out of sight and then slowly exhaled. I was dizzy, though if it was from holding my breath or from the sheer fear I felt, I wasn't sure. I was grateful that I hadn't brought Sandy with me; I didn't want her in the cross-hairs of supernatural assassins.

I turned back around and walked back through the zoo. The animals were starting to freak out, screaming and bouncing around their cages and enclosures. Now that the Ser'im were gone, they were feeling brave enough to work through the anxiety that the unnatural things brought with them. Approaching Mitchell and Cathy, I waved my hand absently.

"You all right there, Ze'ev?" Mitchell asked. "You look like you seen a ghost."

I laughed at that—I could deal with a dybbuk, that was no problem. I shook my head and sighed, getting my bearings. They didn't need to know the truth; they didn't need to know that unnatural demons from somewhere else had invaded our reality and slaughtered animals at their zoo just to get my attention.

"The monsters are gone," I said instead. At least that was true.

"What the hell were those things then?" Mitchell asked; a fair question, but not one I was prepared to explain to a couple of lay people.

"Just cryptids. They don't tend to be spotted very often, but I ran them off. I'll put down some wards around the zoo to keep them out, but uh, judging by what they did in your wolf exhibit, I don't think you'll be able to open today."

"And your wards will keep them out?" Cathy asked. She was still crying; I didn't blame her.

"Yeah, they won't be back."

I didn't know if my wards would do anything at all, actually, but I didn't think the Ser'im would come back here. They had come here to make a point. My name meant wolf, and they killed a bunch of wolves near where I had fought a werewolf. They wanted me to know they knew everything about me, they wanted me to know they were more dangerous than Stübbe had been. The truth was, though, I knew precious little about the Ser'im. I would need to research, try to understand what they wanted—other than my death.

"I'll get started on that," I offered and pushed past Mitchell and Cathy. They would have to deal with cleaning up the terrible mess the demons had made while I walked the perimeter of the zoo and did what I could to protect it from further supernatural threat.

After putting up what amounted to some blessings and folk tale wards around the zoo, I went home and crashed. I was beat. It felt like no matter what was happening, it all happened at once. Vampire, Sheyd, Ser'im, it was almost comical how much things piled up. But after everything that had happened in the last

24 hours, I needed to sleep. I could deal with it all on the other side.

Chapter 5

Even after I moved away, trips to Crisp were a favorite. I had friends who lived there, and when I was a kid, the long drive just meant playing my Game Boy for a few hours while annoying my sisters. I didn't make the trip much as an adult. After adolescence, I didn't want to interact with the angel hidden in the barn. That probably sounds odd, but being in that barn, despite the presence of a literal angel, was always unsettling, terrifying. And not in the awe-struck being in the presence of the divine sort of way but as a cold, terrifying chill that permeated everything. As though the angel was incidental, as if the angel was merely the lure of some terrible deep-sea angler waiting to devour me. That was why I didn't go back, that was why I didn't ask Domah for help or advice.

So why was I in Crisp now? I took a step forward, watching the small town fly past me with each step until I stood in front of the barn. It made a certain kind of sense really. I was facing demons, not a monster or spirit that people called demons but actual demons. I needed to do research, needed to delve into older books, possibly even proscribed books, to find the knowledge I would need to combat the threat of the Ser'im.

My head was fuzzy. I couldn't remember driving here, but here I stood. I must have struck out in my research and it only left the one option. I had to turn to Domah, angel of silence, to figure out a way to survive, not just survive but end the demonic threat the Ser'im posed. And I had to do all of that while also trying to untangle the mystery of Isingway's missing brother. It made sense that I had come here. Returned to this dilapidated barn set way back on a dirt path off a back road in one of the smallest towns in America. The fact that I didn't remember the journey just meant that I had exhausted myself on research.

I pushed the large sliding door of the barn to the side, allowing daylight to illuminate the inside.

Nothing had changed. Dust, dirt, and cobwebs covered every surface. The world inside the barn was stuck in time, a disparate reality from the outside world. I felt like I was walking through molasses as I entered, like each step was impossibly heavy. At the same time, I couldn't stop. My feet seemed set to move of their own volition, carrying me further into the musty interior. I passed the corpse of a cow that had died before I was born and was now just a loose collection of bones. I almost laughed to myself. In my dreams when I came here, I was so scared, so timid. But in reality, when I was in control, I could just jaunt past the cobwebs and dead cow and the desiccated man in the fine Italian suit on my way to the back door.

I reached for the handle of the back door, the door that would lead me to where Domah rested, where I had originally found him and the *other thing*. But before I could grasp the handle, the sounds of sandpaper ripping startled me. I whirled in place and faced the terrifyingly ancient man in the black suit. A wilted tulip jutted from his lapel, and he was painful to look at. His skin was so tight against his skull that it was stretched to near translucence. I could see the blue, watery blood in his veins. His eyes were just as weak and watery, covered in a film like a walking corpse from a horror film. I opened my mouth, but nothing came out but a wheeze. I realized that my throat had closed in terror. I was horrified by this man.

The sound I had heard had been him clearing his throat.

"Ruins ... you aren't supposed to go into ruins alone," he finally stated. His voice was the etching of diamonds against glass.

I stared at him. He was human, or at least human adjacent, but I didn't know what he was exactly, and I didn't have any weapons with me.

"I'm not going to any ruins," I finally managed, but the old man just raised his painfully thin arms and gestured to the dilapidated barn around us.

"You think that ruins must be stone and ancient," he said. "But ruins can be any empty building that has fallen into … ruin." He gave me a sly look, which I hated. "Tell me, do you know why it is written that one should avoid ruins?"

"It isn't avoiding ruins, it's avoiding going alone or with a woman," I clarified, my years of Daf Yomi and studying Talmud with Nathan flooding back into my memory. "And you avoid ruins because there could be robbers or you might be accused of sleeping with the woman. I think we're pretty well past worrying about the latter. Are you here to rob me?"

"You're missing one reason," the man said, his rictus grin making my own mouth hurt.

"Because the Sheydim hide in ruins. You aren't Sheyd." I don't know how I knew that, I just did. In the church, when I had spotted Isingway, I had tapped into an awareness fueled by adrenaline and training that had allowed me to see Isingway's aura. Seeing is probably the wrong word; I sensed it, felt it. The Sheydim have an aura like a stain, something that isn't quite natural, not a part of the natural order of things. I didn't feel anything from the old man. No darkness, no shadow, no oddness, no light or life. It was as if the ghastly man in the suit simply didn't exist. Despite my bluster, I also knew that I didn't know enough; he could be a demon or just something completely outside the scope of my knowledge.

"Technically, the Talmud warns against the malik'im, and with good reason. In places like this, the malik'im, lilit'im, Ser'im, here they can find you, even here." His voice rasped on like tape being ripped from an old cardboard box. "But before you ask, I am not of them either. But I would not open that door, Ze'ev Moshe Kaplan, I would not continue on your path."

I frowned. My hand was still on the handle to the door outside, to where Domah was waiting. It was strange that he hadn't come in, that he hadn't heard us speaking. I suddenly felt anxious, like the terrible man had done something to the angel. I turned the handle and pulled, yanking the door open. A vast emptiness lay beyond, not the little gated area, not the angel, not the terrible thing that had once been there. Just a mind-shredding emptiness of nothing that made my heart and soul ache.

"What ..." I gasped, but then I made something out in the distance within the void. A dot that rose and grew larger as it seemed to come closer. It was a mountain suspended in nothingness, a stony geography that was as impossible in the scope of its size as its existence in empty space. Around the planet sized mountain, as though it had a gravitational pull of its own, I saw several lifeless moons circling in dread orbit. In that void, there was no light or darkness, no stars, no meaning. This was a place where those concepts ceased to have any meaning at all. As the mountain came closer, filling my sight, I realized it was covered in chains, and in those chains …

"Fuck!" I screamed as I shot up in bed, drenched in cooling sweat.

The dream. The dream about Crisp and the barn. I hated that dream; I hated the way deja vu flooded my brain as I woke up and thought about it. It was taught that any dream was a gift from G-d. If that were the case, I wish I could get the receipt for this one, exchange it so that I could stop going back to the worst day of my life over and over again. There had been something different, though. I remembered a mountain, and speaking to … someone. But the dream was already fading. I sighed and reached over to turn the bedside lamp on and looked around my bedroom. My apartment, a little one bedroom on the south side of Austin, was messy. I hadn't really been giving it the love it needed to be livable. Almost all my time had been spent trying to teach a couple of kids or trying to diplomatically defuse the situation with Sara.

I grabbed my phone to check the time. I had actually slept in, which was nice, but I also had several texts from Sara. Wincing, I flicked them open. To my surprise, she was just asking if I wanted to get dinner. No snark, no hostility. It immediately made me suspicious. But I wanted to see her, I wanted to work through all of this, I did love her. I messaged back

-*I would love to see you, come by your place? We can cook?*

-*No.* She responded, followed immediately by -*I want to go out, lets go to Kerbey.*

A nice safe option. I felt my heart sinking. She wanted to be in public, definitely no make-up sex, no intimacy or chance to just hash it out. She wanted to meet in public, at a restaurant. Maybe she didn't want me making a scene. I shot back the affirmative and promised to meet her at eight. I was just being paranoid. Sara liked going to restaurants, she enjoyed going out, more than I did anyway. She was always either at home or at the hospital where she worked, so going out was a treat for her. Unlike me, who ended up eating out for most meals while driving around the city. Rivka had once offered to do meal prep for me, probably how she stayed in such great shape, but I hadn't been willing to give up my mid-week enchiladas and burgers, not yet anyway.

I glanced back down at the phone in my hand, looking at the time I had already checked. Despite wanting to go back to sleep, I needed to get moving. So long as I wanted to continue eating cheese enchiladas and burgers, which I did want, I also needed to work out so that my heart didn't give out next time some terrible monster was chasing me. I grabbed some shorts, my kindle, and an old IDF t-shirt before heading out the door. The gym was within walking distance, most things on this side of Riverside, of the river, and I-35 were, and it was cool enough that I wouldn't have a heatstroke getting there.

An hour or so later, I was finishing up my cardio, reading through a study on early Israelites before they had settled, and listening to some mindless thrumming music. One of the most amazing things I had learned was how disparate the stereotypes of Jews were. Here in Texas, people always imagined Woody Allen, sheepish East Coast guys with no back bone. The idea of the Jewish people being hardy nomads whose rituals were as in-line with shamanism as anything else was a completely alien concept.

I was nasty and sweaty now, but at least I had forgotten all about the nightmare. I could think clearly. I looked back at my phone; no new messages from Sara. My anxiety picked at me. Anxiety was nothing new, but it was never helpful. I walked back home, scrolling through my phone, trying to distract myself from the existential dread that hung over me.

I considered my relationship with Sara. She was amazing, a nurse, loving, intelligent, sweet, funny … She walked the line of being beautiful, sexy, and cute all at once and drove me wild. I was lucky to have her. But she wasn't lucky to have me. I mean, I suppose I'm attractive enough, for the average guy, she told me she loved my green eyes, but I was always busy, never available. Really, her terrible work schedule was probably the only reason we had lasted together as long as we had, that and her trusting nature. Not that I had ever walked around on her, but I did lie. I lied constantly. Not out of any malice, not because I wanted to lie to her, but because I couldn't tell her the truth. I couldn't just tell her, *Hey, I'm out hunting monsters tonight,* or, *Don't wait up, I'm tracking down the last members of a necromantic cult.* It just didn't work. My life, my real life, was incompatible with a healthy relationship.

Sara thought I was a youth leader and instructor for the Central Conference of American Reform Rabbis. Technically, my paychecks did come from that group, I think on the paperwork I was listed as a prayer leader. But the truth was that my bosses were a group called the Beit Din, scholars and leaders who understood the monstrous nature of reality and oversaw myself and other Jewish monster hunters and exorcists. My immediate supervisor, Nathan, didn't approve of my relationship with Sara, he considered it treif. She wasn't religious, we weren't married, all of that. I'm sure if given the chance, he would try to set me up with some nice Jewish girl in the know, but the last thing I wanted was Nathan mucking about in my personal life.

When I got home, I got in the shower and started planning my day around dinner with Sara. She was a good thing in my life, I didn't want to lose her, and I needed to do whatever it took to prove I was serious and intended to keep her. I needed to lay down boundaries with Nathan, with work. It wasn't something they would like, hell, I didn't know if it was something that was allowed. But if I wanted to keep my relationship with Sara, or if I wanted a healthy relationship of any sort with anyone, I needed to be able to live a normal life. It was a myth that the things that went bump in the night weren't around during the day, and a dybbuk could be exorcised during any hour. It's just that people tended to be more aware of the strange when there was less stimuli. The world was a noisy, bright place, and the ambient sights and sounds of the day time drowned out the presence of the unusual.

It did make my job easier, hunting at night; fewer people to question what the fuck I was doing, fewer hapless civilians to get caught in some sort of mystical crossfire. But again, that didn't mean it couldn't happen during the day. Hell, I had summoned a Sheyd and hunted down Stübbe during the middle of the day. And the Ser'im showed themselves in public in the middle of the day without giving a single damn about the humans that saw them. I could be a day shift sort of guy, I just had to figure out how to make that demand. That was a challenge in and of itself.

I had a few hours before I was going to meet with Sara at Kerbey Lane Cafe, and it wasn't very far, so I had some time to kill. I considered doing research. I needed to figure out what I could find out about the Ser'im; I also needed to figure out what happened to Oronymous, Isingway's brother. Just the thought of the demons and the Sheydim made my stomach twist in knots. I decided that I needed to start drawing boundaries right here and now. Even if they were only boundaries for myself.

I grabbed my worn out meditation cushion and tossed it on the floor. I bought it in Nepal years ago, and despite the fact that there was nothing particularly special about it—and that I could literally meditate anywhere, at any time—the cushion held a special place in my heart. I sunk down on it, feeling the well-worn grooves from years of use, closed my eyes, and began a soft chant. There are countless ways to meditate, and different forms of meditation can be used to focus intention in different ways. Right then, though, I just wanted to clear my head, I wanted to focus on what was really important to me in that moment, I wanted to be mindful. I chanted the word *Hineni*.

Hineni means "here I am." It shows up a few times in the Torah but is most noticeable when G-d asks Abraham and Moses where they are and they respond with "Hineni." On the surface, it's a bit ridiculous. Why would G-d ask that question? But I think it's not a question at all but a call to action. Hineni, in these cases, is not about where they are physically. When Moses responds with Hineni, he means he is present, in the moment, that his attention is focused, that he has kavanagh. Hineni is about not being scattered, not thinking about the future, not being swallowed by the past, but being aware of the surrounding reality enough that you can actually begin being. I would need that; not only would I need it but I owed Sara that. I owed her being completely in the moment with her, listening, responding, interacting, not with my fears or my hopes but with her in her entirety. Hineni.

Meditation is an art made efficient with practice, one that couldn't be perfected. But I had a lot of practice. I allowed hours to slip away while meditating. My mind turned over Sara and our relationship. I could see my shortcomings easily, and every time my thoughts ventured into the reasons for those shortcomings, I gently brought my mind back. Because it didn't matter, at all, what my reasons were. It didn't matter if I was saving lives, or fighting the good fight, or anything else I told myself. Because she didn't see any of that. All she saw was all the times I canceled plans, all the times I wasn't available, or the times I was distracted. I needed to prioritize her if I was going to keep her. If it wasn't already too late. I pushed that thought out of my head; it just wasn't helpful.

Eventually, I rose and shook myself out of the meditative state. It was time to meet up with Sara.

Chapter 6

Kerbey Lane wasn't a fancy restaurant, but I still tried to dress up a little—slacks, button up, and a sports coat. I also swung by the local HEB grocery store and grabbed a bouquet of flowers. Lilies, Sara's favorite. I was trying. I got there early and found a booth seat where I could see the door when Sara came in. Getting there early, flowers, something approaching a suit. I could be a nice Jewish boy when I tried. It was just hard to find time to try, what with work specifically paying me to not be very nice. I frowned and pulled my mind away from my damned excuses again.

There she was. She was not dressed up; she was in sweat pants and a t-shirt. Her fine blond hair was up in a messy bun, and I could see she had only put on the bare minimum of makeup she needed to feel comfortable going out. Despite all that, she was so beautiful and sexy to me. She was taller than average and never slouched. She looked like she had learned to walk in a modeling school where they forced her to walk with books on her head. She was lithe, too tall to be a ballerina, but long and slender. The first time I had met her, I had assumed she was a model doing charity work for some brand, or maybe an actress researching a role as a nurse.

Of course, I met her in the hospital. I had gotten on the wrong side of a zar, a djinn like spirit that had possessed a massive alleycat in order to steal the breath of sleeping children. I managed to carry the day but ended up in the hospital for my trouble. Despite me being a man hospitalized for getting my ass kicked by a cat, Sara had been sweet, kind, and didn't spend too much time teasing me. When I was discharged, I found her and asked her to dinner. That had been nearly five years ago, and we had our ups and downs. More ups, I thought; but at the same time, lately, there had definitely been more downs.

I rose and waved; she rewarded me with a tight-lipped smile. She was tense, and I could feel the ice cold lump of fear rising from my gut and into my throat. I pushed it back down, intent on not seeming desperate or despondent.

"Hi there," I offered softly, presenting the flowers to her.

She took them and inhaled the fragrance, some of the tightness leaving her face as she enjoyed them. She sighed and opened her beautiful blue eyes, regarding me with something between frustration and affection. I clung to that affection, putting all of my hopes in that one thing. She sat down in the booth I had grabbed us and slid down, setting the flowers down before flipping the menu open.

I slid into the booth across from her, mirroring her movements. "I missed you."

"Did you?" she asked on the heels of my statement, as if the question had been locked and loaded on her lips before she even stepped foot out her door this morning.

I started to answer, but she cut me off with a wave of her hand and closed the menu. "I know you'll tell me you have, I know you'll say that you wanted to call me, to see me. Maybe you did." She shrugged. "But how would I know that?"

"I'm telling you now."

"And do you know what telling me something with no actual action means? To me?"

"Nothing?" I answered. It felt like I was trapped in a script. Sara had her lines and she wouldn't accept anything but the appropriate responses from me.

"Less," she corrected.

"I'm sorry, Sara. I don't ever want you to feel like you aren't important."

"Luckily for me, my sense of self-worth isn't tied to how good of a boyfriend you are. Unfortunately, my patience with you is. I know you intend to do nice things, I know you intend to show me you care, but the road to hell is paved with good intentions, a healthy relationship isn't."

I winced at the analogy, and not only because it was about as opposite from my own theology and philosophy as possible but because I knew what she was doing, and I didn't see a lot of paths towards escaping the inevitable. "Sara, I know these last few months have been hard, but I am—"

"Last few months? Ze'ev, look at our relationship. It started fine, but the majority is you coming over, we eat, we have sex, and then we don't see each other or talk until the next time one of us decides we want sex more than we want to avoid one another."

"I never want to avoid you, Sara." I didn't want to even acknowledge that she had said she wanted to avoid me.

"That isn't how you act, and yeah, the sex is good, really good, but I need more out of a relationship than that. I need commitment, I need to be your priority, and it isn't the first time I've told you that."

"You have, and I want more than sex too. I don't think of you as a fuck-buddy or a booty call, you're my girlfriend. I love you." I put those words out there like an armchair reactionary flying the flag on their porch: performative, perfunctory, desperate.

She looked at me, her eyes boring into mine with barely disguised exhaustion. "I told you before, I'm a G-ddamned catch. Do you know how many men hit on me a day?"

"Patients?"

"Patients, doctors, lawyers, family of patients; and every time, I tell them that while I'm flattered, I have a boyfriend. It's feeling more like a lie every time. At least if I was with a doctor, I could have some money on top of being neglected." She smiled, but I couldn't tell if it was because of her joke or because she was trying not to cry.

"Well, I'm not ever going to be wealthy, Sara. I'm never going to be a lawyer or a doctor or anything like that, but I do care about you, deeply, and I want to be with you. I know that you don't feel like I deserve another chance, but, but I want to ask you for one. Just one."

"One?" she asked. Her eyes dug into my soul, it reminded me of the way Lillith had torn into my soul and mind in the City East-of-Nod.

Involuntarily, my body shuddered at the memory, arousal and fear swimming into my brain. I closed my eyes, blocking out the sensation, centering myself before reopening my eyes and meeting Sara's intense gaze.

"One," I answered. I had to prove myself. I had to make this right, if she would let me. And I knew I could do it, I knew I could be a better boyfriend, a partner, more than some fuck-boy that disappointed her over and over again. I knew I could find balance; I could find some path that would allow me to walk the line.

I thought about Rivkah, Sandy, and Anthony. I could train any of them to fight monsters, to face demons and Sheydim, but that would just be passing on this lifestyle. It would be hoisting my responsibility on someone else, and I couldn't do that either. How much of this was destiny and fate, and how much was a self-fulfilling curse? "I know you've given me more chances than I'm even aware of, Sara—"

"More than you know," she agreed.

"And I know I don't deserve another chance. But I'm asking for it anyway, and if I fuck it up, then ... then we'll both know that I didn't deserve you." I trailed off. I didn't like talking that way, but I didn't know how else to put my cards on the table.

Sara stared at me, the hardness in her eyes was cold and dominating. She was silent for several moments before she let out a huge sigh and held up a finger. "Okay. One chance. But I want you to know it isn't for your sake, or because you're cute or good in bed. I'm giving you one more chance because I think it would honestly break Toof's heart if you didn't come by anymore."

Toof was her English bulldog; he was a nearly spherical mound of skin, drool, and fat, and he was a good boy. I made a mental note to get him some steak for earning me my 100th chance.

I nodded and smiled. I reached across the table for Sara, and after a moment's thought, she extended her hand and wrapped her fingers in mine. With her free hand, she grabbed her menu and started looking through pages. I don't know how she maintained any appetite after the solid, painful conversation, but I had to guess it was because as a nurse, she had to take care of herself even after the most harrowing encounters. I watched her looking over the menu before glancing down at mine, stroking her fingers, finding comfort in that moment while I tried to summon some sort of appetite.

"Okay." Sara broke my concentration suddenly. "One chance. My parents are coming to town next week. You've always dodged the bullet of meeting them. You want to prove you're serious, you come to dinner with us, you prove you're actually boyfriend material, capiche?"

"Understood," I agreed immediately, even if everything inside of me shrunk up. I had avoided meeting her parents so far. Parents were always so full of questions, questions that meant I had to keep the sprawling network of lies and deceit I had built around my life straight. One false move and everything I had done and built, as well as my second chance with Sara, would be destroyed. "I can't wait," I said, looking down at the menu to hide the fear in my eyes.

"I'm not blind, Ze'ev, I know you don't want to meet them; but that's what relationships mean, doing things you don't always want to do because your partner does. It means being honest and it means sacrifice. I want to know you can handle both of those things."

I looked back up and nodded in agreement. "I can." I squeezed her hand, hopefully exuding more confidence than I was feeling.

After that, we tried to make small talk, tried to chat, but it was hard. There were two elephants in the room. One was obvious, we both knew that Sara had come here to break up with me, that everything depended on my behavior now, on that one chance; and I think we both knew that even if I nailed that, it would be hard to salvage a relationship. But I loved her, and I had to fight for it. The other elephant, the one Sara wasn't aware of, was the lies. Small talk consisted of chatting about what we had been up to, about work, about everything we had been doing instead of seeing each other. And I couldn't tell her the truth.

Even now, when everything was on the line, I had to lie. It was exhausting and painful, and I hated every second of it. But the only other option I could have was telling Sara the truth, and then not only would she not believe me, she would know that almost everything I had told her about myself had been a lie too. I was trapped in a spiderweb of my own deceit, unable to find a way to get to the truth.

Somehow, though, we got through dinner. We kissed, we said goodbye, and I promised to meet her for dinner with her parents. I stood outside the Kerbey for a while after she walked away, watching her get in her car and drive off into the night. I felt cold, I felt hopeless and sad. I just wanted to go home and collapse in my bed and not move until it was time to get ready to meet her parents.

"There you are."

I winced at the sound of the clipped voice before turning to look at Isingway.

"How long have you been there?" I asked, maybe more accusation in that question than intended, but I didn't like the idea of this Sheyd, or any Sheydim for that matter, following me around. Especially when I was handling painful and personal business.

"Not long, I spoke as I approached." He paused, eying me. "Why, have you been doing something suspicious?"

"Everything I do is suspicious to someone, Isingway, but I do like my privacy." I shrugged; no matter how I felt, it was time to get to work. "How about Oro? Oro do anything suspicious?"

"Everything we Sheydim do is suspicious to someone, Ze'ev," he answered with a smirk. He had a point.

"Okay, well, was he involved in anything he shouldn't have been from our perspective?"

"Oro loved being involved with humans. He loved working as a cop, he felt it was his own path to Olam Ha-ba. His own tikkun olam."

I wasn't surprised to hear that even the Sheydim were concerned about Olam Ha-ba, the world to come. It was heaven, in a way. It was what the world would become when the messiah showed up. A return to the garden of Eden, a time and place of no conflict. It was also all there was. You either secured your place in the world to come or you existed in a dull limbo, or maybe you were reabsorbed into the divine nothingness. But there was nothing to aim for in a spiritual sense other than Olam Ha-ba. And the point of life, at least for us lesser mortals, was tikkun olam, the healing of the world. Tikkun olam would bring about the messianic age faster, bring us closer to the world to come so that we could all just … I don't know, be happy, I hope.

"Well, being a cop isn't the *easiest* way to do good," I said. Isingway screwed his face up tight—in an age of ACAB and defund the police, it was difficult to see police work as tikkun olam. "But, did he keep a house? Somewhere we can check out?"

Isingway nodded, deciding for the time being that discussing human politics and turmoil might not be the best use of his time. "Why don't you drive," he said. "I'll direct you."

It wasn't a far drive. It turned out Oro had been living downtown. I thought about making a remark about how likely it was that an honest cop could afford an apartment in downtown Austin, but I decided against it. It just didn't help my cause to disparage Isingway's brother, that and making suppositions about the finances of beings that were immortal shape-changers was probably hopeless. We parked on the street, paid the meter, and headed up. From the way Isingway was craning his neck to look around, I had to assume he hadn't actually been here before.

"So …" I said as we got in the elevator. "Why me? Do the Sheydim not have their own police? I'm not a detective, there are better people to call than me."

"I told you, you're the last person I know was with Oro, the last person to see him."

"Right, but don't you have resources I don't?" I pressed.

Isingway glanced at me without moving his head, giving me wicked side eye. "The truth is our peace keepers are terrifying. I don't want Bel involved unless he has to be. Our 'detectives' are more akin to tracking hounds. The prince and the queen have little time for dissonance in their kingdom. Too many wars have been fought among my kind. So, if I discover that Oro's disappearance has something to do with intrigue or Sheydim politics, I can work through that before getting some heavy hitter involved; if I involve other Sheydim, I lose control of the situation immediately. If not, his disappearance is more …" He trailed off a moment. "If something else happened that isn't related to the Sheydim, if it it's something human, then I want to have a human with a strong understanding of magic with me. We aren't like you in a lot of ways, but in a lot of ways we are. Passion, we have passion, and we can be overzealous. But in the end, Ze'ev, I just want my brother back."

My first instinct was to be a smartass, but I squelched it. I had two sisters, and I know I would do anything to make sure they were safe and sound. Including working with someone I didn't want to work with. I also remembered Alex. He was a cop. He could have easily have gotten help in the office, but he had come to me. He had wanted revenge. I wondered if Isingway was looking to deal his own form of justice.

"Yeah, we'll find him, Isingway, we'll find your brother." I wasn't sure, of course; I couldn't be. But I would try my hardest to fulfill my part of this bargain. I wondered if that would make me square with the six fingered figure who had sent me through the portal when I needed to rescue Sandy. I could hope, but I had a sinking feeling that it wouldn't amount to much. Once in debt to inhuman forces, it was pretty much guaranteed that you would be embroiled with them until you died. After all, they were ancient beings adept at manipulation. I could only really hope that, after this, I would be beneath the notice of whatever forces held my IOU slip.

Isingway, unaware of my internal dialog, nodded and stepped off the elevator. I followed him through the hallway until we reached Oro's apartment. I paused, waiting for him to produce a key, but instead, he simply walked through the door as though it wasn't there at all. Sheyd could do that, they could choose to be immaterial, touch but be untouched. I stared at the closed door for a few moments, wondering if he was going to let me in or not. After several minutes standing alone in the hallway, I sighed, reached forward, and turned the doorknob. The door swung open effortlessly. It hadn't been locked.

Isingway looked up at me from where he stood amidst a chaotic mess. "This is not how Oro would live," he said simply.

"It looks like there was a struggle," was all I could really say in response as I stepped into the apartment and closed the door behind me.

The place was wrecked. Broken furniture, belongings scattered everywhere. I stepped over a pile of shattered plates and stopped beside Isingway. "I'm surprised nothing was reported."

Isingway didn't respond, stepping away and sifting through the debris that was left of his brother's life. I considered helping, trying to look for clues, but the truth was I didn't know anything about Oro, I didn't know what would or wouldn't be out of place. But I could look beyond the physical. I pushed a pile of scattered books off of the couch and sat down.

For a few moments, I watched Isingway as he moved around, but then I let my eyes lose focus and instead concentrated on my breathing. I considered each breath as it came in, filling me, and each exhale that took out the bad air. The air I breathed in was thick with energy, it was so tangible it almost broke the concentration I was building. But I was well practiced with finding my center in stressful situations, and I brought my mind back to the present. There was something familiar here, something I had felt before, seen before, tasted before.

I rose from the couch, still in a meditative state, and moved through the apartment. I ignored the clutter and debris of a life destroyed and followed the faint lines of power and magic that swirled around me. I wondered if Isingway could sense them. Maybe all of this energy was simply because it was the dwelling of one of the Sheydim. It was a funny thought, though, a downtown loft being the home of an ancient creature from myth.

Could they even sense magic? Could they see auras and energy and power? Or as beings of power, were they blind to the energy that surrounded all things? I didn't know. I paused next to a wall. My eyes, still unfocused, ignoring reality, touched the arcane symbol that had been burned into the doorway. It left no mark on the physical world, but the spiritual plane was marred. Like an image on gossamer set over the lens of reality.

The symbol on the door frame was burnt into the soul of the wood, into the very essence of the loft. An invocation of silence. That was why no one had called the cops. It was the main source of the magic swirling around the loft, but not the only one. There was something else here too, creating a subtle whirlwind warp in the energies. I stepped away from the wall, my eyes half closed, and my eyes unfocused as I traced the patterns of swirling energy in the air. As softly as

I could, I hummed a niggun, a wordless prayer; the sound was comforting. The low hum vibrated through my throat and wrapped around me like a blanket of familiarity. The sound was an energy of its own, something that interacted with the metaphysical world I was attempting to keep my gaze on.

The niggun is a tangible thing, though we rarely see or understand that. Have you ever sung a song in a large group? It's why Christian youth camps do it, it's why congregations all over the world pray in melody. It makes people weep, it strengthens the bond of community and shared experience. So much so that the sound of those melodies can trigger that sense of community even when you are alone. The niggun is even better. It transcends language and words, it's a chant, a song, and a hymn all at once that anyone can learn almost immediately. Being a wordless chant meant that it could be sung during prayer, during meditation, during worship, or during mindless work, all without interrupting the kavanagh of what you were doing.

I watched the tendrils of my niggun wrap around me in the spiritual world, though "world" was the wrong word. It wasn't like there were two existences on top of one another. Rather, the world of spirits, angels, and magic was the same world we occupied, but it could only be seen through the lens of an altered state. Throughout the ages, men had used different means to attain this sight: starvation, flagellation, drugs, or just fervent prayer. I had tried the drugs and fasting angle myself, but I found that altering my state through hunger made me too ornery to get much done, and drugs made it hard for me to focus my intention once I could observe the power behind our reality.

I concentrated on the sounds of the niggun, on the way its hum vibrated through my neck and against my teeth. I could see the whisper of blue energy thrumming with the rhythm of the melody as it stretched throughout the loft and sought out the source of the warping of natural power. I followed the strands of power, lost in my own niggun. I probably looked drunk, eyes half closed, hands raised and moving in time with my slurred wordless song as I half-danced, half-walked through the loft. But my song worked, and I found myself staring down at the couch.

"I found something!" I called as I crouched down and pulled the cushion up.

The blade clattered to the floor. It was a long, curved dagger with a bit of red silk tied to the handle. I recognized it immediately. I had seen dozens like it. It was the calling card of the Thuggee, an ancient cult of Kali who spread theft and murder across ancient India. They had at one point gone to ground, thought to be completely extinct, and maybe they were. Maybe those who still carried these daggers were no longer worshipers of Kali. After all, Kali wasn't the G-ddess of death, or of undeath, and everyone I knew who had carried one of these had been a necromancer or aspired to be one. This dagger was a clear calling card, and it pointed to an impossible truth.

"We need to go pay a visit to Basken in prison; he's behind this," I said, hating the words even as they left my lips.

Chapter 7

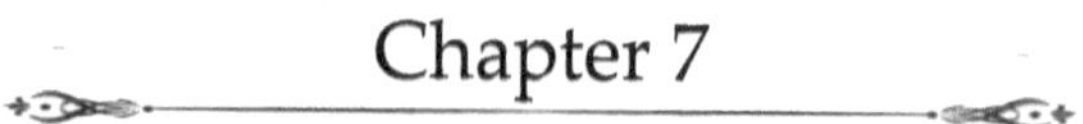

I called Alex Barman while driving out towards Del Valle's Travis County Correctional Complex. It rang twice before he answered.

"Ze'ev?" he asked. He sounded tired, which seeing as I was calling him near 6:00 a.m. wasn't super shocking. "What, what's up?" For years, Alex had been an acquaintance from shul, someone I would run into before services and we would share a quick word. He had become someone I could point towards any illegal activity I ran into during the course of my job. Then, some months ago, Alex's daughter had been killed by a werewolf named Stübbe, the same werewolf that Isingway's brother took on with me. I had dealt with Stübbe and avenged his daughter's death. All below the table. During the course of that, Alex had learned the truth about what I do and what the world was really like.

"Hey, Alex, how are you? How's your wife?" I asked, trying to be cordial.

"Fine, what do you need?"

I would be hurt by the assumption I wouldn't call if I didn't need something if it weren't so accurate. Amanda, a witch from the local magic shop, had once compared me to the boy from the Giving Tree story. Maybe that was something I should work on.

"Yeah, I need to interview Oliver Basken. I'm on my way to lock-up now."

"What? You can't just go and talk to Basken. That's, no, man," Alex responded immediately. "What the hell would make you think you could do that?"

"Remember when those two cultists attacked me outside my workshop?" I asked.

"Yeah," he responded hesitantly. I realized he probably hadn't put the pieces together that Basken was an actual sorcerer until that moment.

"Well, I don't think his cult's wiped up entirely." I paused, glancing at Isingway in the passenger seat. "I'm following up on a missing person I'm looking for, and I found evidence of the cult. The only lead I have is with Basken."

"Missing person. Isn't this the sort of thing you should leave to me and the police?"

I shrugged a little, despite the fact he couldn't see me.

"No, this falls pretty heavily into my purview, Alex." I let him digest that. "So does Basken; but since Basken is human and committed actual prosecutable crimes, I figured we had joint custody." I grinned at my own joke, but Alex didn't laugh.

"I'm not going to fight for jurisdiction with you, Ze'ev." His voice was flat; he was annoyed, but I could tell he also knew what sort of stakes I dealt in. "Look, I'll see what I can do. Basken is high profile, he's a big deal, and he's still awaiting trial, so a lot of eyes will be on him." There was another long pause before I heard the sigh that meant I had won him over—I knew I would. "Seeing as you were part of the whole ordeal with him … I think I can manage it, just … I'll meet you there."

I winced. I didn't want Barman with me while I interviewed Basken, but I realized there might not be another way. "Thanks, see you in a bit." I hung up.

"Who is Basken, and why are we going to talk to him?" Isingway asked.

"Basken was the leader of a cult, a bunch of necromancers here in Texas that made some trouble for me. Basically dragged me into a lot of really bad shit, got me mixed up with ghouls and dybbukim." I thought about Sandy and Kristine. Kristine had been a victim of the cult, her skull crushed by some malevolent force inhabiting a statue. I had destroyed the statue, but I doubted that did anything to the thing that had been animating it. "Anyway, the dagger with the silk tied to it was sort of a calling card of theirs. So is home invasion. My first brush with them was when they broke into my home and tried to kill me with one of those knives."

"But the man is in prison now?"

"Yeah, I cut the tendons in his hand so he couldn't use magic anymore and pretty much delivered him to the cops." I decided not to mention the turf war I had set off between ghouls and Basken's cult, the death, the destruction, or the way I had shot at police in order to lure the cops into the clearing where said turf war was being waged. None of that was really pertinent to what we were doing now, at least I hoped it wouldn't be.

"So how would ..."

"Assuming someone has lost power because they're in prison would be a mistake. I don't know how the Sheydim do things, but when humans go to prison, they often still have connections to the outside world, they form gangs, and smuggle. The truth is that our prison system does dick all to stop really powerful people and fucks over the lightest offenders. If Basken's cult is still operating, it's a sure guess that Basken himself is somehow pulling the strings behind it, or at least knows who would have taken over." I said it all with a straight face, but inside I was fuming. How the fuck did I miss more cultist? I had spent the better part of a year tracking down members of Basken's cult using traditional and occult methods. Spells and logic, trinkets and late night stake-outs. I thought I had cleared the entire damned nest out.

"I have another question," Isingway stated calmly— though maybe a bit timidly, maybe I was being more snappish than I had realized. "Why would he share any information with you?" It was a good question, one I had been trying to wrap my mind around. I didn't exactly have easy leverage, but I would think of something. I was good at bluffing—at least I thought I was.

"I'll handle that. You'll wait for me outside, though, maybe invisibly."

"Why would I do that?" Isingway pressed, obviously irritated by the idea of being sidelined.

"Because if Baskin had something to do with it and you go ape-shit and kill him or anyone else in the prison and then ghost, I'll be left to deal with the aftermath. I'll lose everything and everyone I care about. So you'll wait the fuck outside, and I'll fill you in after I'm done," I explained patiently. I totally understood his irritation, and honestly, I would understand any anger or violence he brought to bear. But I had to watch out for myself; I couldn't let Isingway cost me everything.

He turned back to stare ahead as we pulled into the correctional facility—a friendly way of saying prison, jail, or county lock up, but they were all the same thing. Cogs in the machine of the powerful, you put in the poor and desperate and got free labor out of it. It wasn't a great system. I knew it, Alex knew it, everyone knew it. But at the same time, the only other way I could have dealt with Basken would have been murder. We needed some way to neutralize and segregate true threats and menaces. Preferably without using it as a tool for race and class segregation. I shook my head clear of political thoughts. I didn't have it in me to try to change the system right now, I just needed to get in there and meet up with Basken.

I spotted Alex waiting for me and turned to Isingway to tell him to wait in the car, but he was gone. Well, probably not gone, but at least no longer visible to human eyes.

I would have to hope Isingway would follow my advice and not come in. I got out of the car and approached Alex. He looked tired, more gray than he had been in the past. He smiled a tight-lipped smile when he saw me. I don't think he blamed me for what happened to his daughter, but I would forever be tied to that loss and to the knowledge that the supernatural existed.

"Hello, Ze'ev," he greeted me as I came close enough. "You're a fucking headache, you know that, right?"

"I've been told, but the particulars always escape me. Why am I a headache?"

"This, here, bringing me out here first thing in the G-ddamned morning."

"You couldn't ask me to wait?" I asked defensively.

"Could I? Who knows with you? As far as I knew, you might be trying to fight a vampire or something." I didn't respond, he had been trying to be flippant. My silence was not as subtle as I was hoping. He narrowed his eyes at me. "There are vampires," he stated.

"There are. I did fight one the other night." Was that only yesterday? I looked away from him. He looked exhausted. "How have you been?" I finally asked.

"Not great, Ze'ev. I lost my daughter, my wife barely speaks to me, and on top of all of that, I now know there's a secret horrible world that I can't do anything about." He crossed his arms over his chest.

"That's my job, not yours. You deal with the shit that you can see, you leave the rest to me and mine. It's how it works, how it's always worked," I said.

He sighed, but nodded and turned to lead the way into the prison.

I glanced over at Alex for the sixth time since I had sat down at the small table. He had wanted to come and sit with me, talk to Basken, but I had convinced him he needed to keep the other guards distracted. Alex had fed them a line about an active investigation into the possible existence of more cultists and further cells. Luckily for both me and Alex, he had actually been working that case, so it didn't feel completely unnatural. Whatever he said, it worked, and I was given access. I wasn't sure how he convinced the prison staff to let me speak to him one on one, but if what I needed to talk to the necromancer about was overheard, it could land me in the loony bin and Alex in a whole heap of trouble.

I kept my hands under the table, despite the presence of pre-chewed gum under the metal tabletop. I don't know why I was nervous, I had dealt a blow to his magical abilities and dismantled his cult. But even with those assurances and the fact that there were cops and other prisoners meeting with lawyers and family in the small hall, I knew better than to assume this meeting would be safe for me.

The door opened, and Oliver Basken, the self-styled Lord of Flesh, master necromancer, and serious pain in my ass, walked in. He was a sunken man. Last time I had seen him in person, he had been wearing black robes and a skull mask, like some sort of cheesy 80s horror movie villain. I watched him approaching my table and silently took in the sight of the broken old man. He was balding and had the atrophied form of people who devoted their entire life to finding power through books. His hand, bearing a large ugly scar, trembled with nerve damage tremors as he sat down across from me and allowed the guard to cuff him to the table. My fingernail dug into the gum under the table as I tried to show little to no emotion on my face.

"Hello, Ollie," I said, trying to sound casual.

He didn't respond. His eyes, red-rimmed and hateful, bored into me. If looks could kill, I would already be one of his zombies enslaved to his will. He sat in silence, glaring at me until the guard moved away.

"Ze'ev. Moses. Kaplan." He spat the name as if it were a curse.

I smiled in response, hiding my nerves, reminding myself that there was nothing for me to fear, even as my fingernail drew circles in the disgusting filth under the table.

"I was hoping you would be dead by now." He hissed the words under his breath, brave, but not so brave as to give the police more fuel for his legal funeral pyre.

"Why should I be dead? Did you think that your followers had the wherewithal to challenge me? That's the problem with evil sorcerers, Ollie, you keep all the power for yourself and then your little minions have no real way of dealing with threats to your little power structure."

We sat in silence for several seconds. His eyes bored into me, and I worked hard to give him nothing he could use against me. After what seemed like an eternity, his shoulders slumped and he looked away.

"Why are you here? Haven't you done enough? Taken enough?"

"How much is a life worth?" I asked in response. "You killed a lot of people to try to hurt me." He shrugged, as if he didn't consider it that important. I sighed and shook my head. "I need to know why one of your followers would kidnap or attack one of the Sheydim." I could tell by his surprised look that he hadn't known before now about Oro, but that look of shock disappeared quickly to be replaced with one of thoughtful consideration. He didn't know the specifics, but he had at least a few ideas as to why someone would.

"We are more wide-spread than you might imagine, more insidious, more powerful—"

I cut him off by yawning. I could tell by the hate in his eyes that my dismissal of his grand speech hurt.

"Spare me the details. I'm talking about your cell, your little posse. What would they want with Sheydim?"

"You call them Sheydim, I call them demons. And there are so many different ways they can be useful, so many different components that one—" He cut himself off this time. He looked at me as though just realizing something. "You, you're an exorcist."

"Why shouldn't I be an exorcist?" I replied, thrown off by the sudden change in his tact.

"You can dispel the ghosts and spirits," he pressed.

I didn't like where this was going, but I wasn't entirely surprised either.

I shrugged a little. "I wouldn't say I dispel anything; I just help those who are lost find peace, find a way home. That's the difference between you and me, Ollie, I'm not trying to control the dead, I'm trying to help them."

He waved my explanation away and shook his head. "I have been beset, my dreams, the spirits of the people I raised, and the ones I killed, they aren't letting me sleep, they torment me every single fucking night. If you can stop them ..." He watched my face, his hope turning into a snarl as I didn't respond. "You said you fucking help find peace, help me find peace! You help me, I help you; that's what you want, right? You want to know what happened to the Sheyd? Well, I can help you, but you have to help me first!"

"Part of Jewish law, the rules I follow, state that communing with the dead isn't allowed. The spirits that are tormenting you, Ollie, aren't lost or confused, they are angry. And not without reason. You made your bed, you have to lie in it. I'm sorry." I wasn't sorry but wasn't sure what else I could say.

He leaned back, his eyes hard and mean. "You think that you're in control here, don't you, Ze'ev? That you have control. Did you think my power was just supernatural? That sending me to prison would shackle me and castrate me?"

In the corners of my eyes, I saw that the guard who Alex had been talking to had led him out of the room, inmates were rising. This was a trap, a set up. It was impressive that Basken had managed to set it up as quickly as he had.

"I will always have the upper hand. I am so happy you came here so I could watch you d—"

I pulled my finger loose from the gum I had been picking at under the table and tapped the sigil I had carved there with my fingernail. The room went black. Not just dark, but pitch black, all light swallowed into nothing. The fluorescent lights were off; the sunlight that had come through the windows was absorbed into the void of inky black malice that consumed the entire visitation room. Strange ephemeral shapes screamed in the darkness, shifting under the veil of shadows. They tore at Basken with spectral claws that burned his soul. I leaned forward in the darkness, whispering just loud enough for Basken to hear over the silent moans of the dead and the panicked shouts from the guards.

"You created this situation where the souls of those you hurt clamor for your pain. A thousand thousand evil angels, each created by an evil committed by you, wait by your right hand for your death, countered only by the minute number of good angels you have created through accidental kindness during your youth. I see them stretched out before me like blades of grass in a field, like drops of water in an ocean. All arrayed against you, all waiting for the moment you slip from life and free will and answer for all you have done. They wait in the shadows of night and nightmare. They breathe your name in each shuddered breath that leaks into our world from theirs. Through a barrier you have made thin. They come for you when the lights are out, Oliver Basken, and my finger is on the fucking light switch."

I leaned back as light was suddenly restored. All around us, tables had been upturned. Guards and inmates had fallen over themselves trying to find safety, trying to find some meaning in the sudden darkness, in the terror within the shadows. Only Basken and I remained seated, and only I was calm. My eyes bored into the necromancer, daring him to make a move, any move. He breathed in shallow gasps, his eyes wide in fear. I hoped it was comparable to the terror he had caused as a free man, that some modicum of vengeance would go to those spirits and ease their suffering. Using magic and invoking an unnatural darkness like that was dangerous, but I had sensed the spirits and entities clamoring for Basken the moment I had approached the prison. All I had done was given him a taste of what was to come, the bitter taste of medicine he had brewed.

"Remember next time you think it would be prudent to come after me," I said calmly, standing up.

No one else rose. Maybe Basken's lackeys were smart enough to realize that this squabble was above their pay grade. More likely, though, they were simply trying to wrap their minds around what just happened. The human mind was an elastic and self-healing organ for the most part. The rigidity of the neural pathways would force the nonbelievers in the crowd to explain away what happened, and the true believers would either keep their mouths shut for fear of being called crazy or *would* be called crazy for their honesty.

I walked to the doors and resisted the urge to turn and look back at Basken. Instead, I waited for them to open the door and let me out. A few minutes later, I was outside with Alex, who was giving me the hairy eyeball.

"What happened in there?" he asked.

"What do you mean?" I asked, trying to play it innocent, but I could tell by the look on his face he was neither impressed nor amused.

"You know what I mean, Ze'ev."

I shrugged. "Nothing. I mean nothing happened with Basken, for all intent and purposes. Basken and I had no issues and made no fuss when the lights went off, everything was fine. And the only people who might trace it back to me or you would either out themselves as being corrupt or sound crazy. So, it's fine, and again, for all intent and purposes, nothing happened." I offered him a tired smile.

"Okay, and what really happened?"

"Basken meddled in forces that no man should control. I just let him know that they wanted to have a word with him. That's all. No one got hurt, no one got in trouble." I paused, considering everything I knew, or more accurately, what I didn't know. The problem was that there was way more magic-related corruption in the justice system than I could have guessed. I belatedly remembered the Sergeant Zalot who set me up in one of Basken's traps, there were the guards who had helped Basken set up his little failed attack in the visiting room, and finally, there was …

"Hey, do you know a uniformed cop by the name of Oscar?" That was Oro's civilian name.

"Not that I can think of. Why?"

"That's my missing person," I admitted. "Only, he isn't a person, not really, he's—"

"My brother," Isingway said as he seemed to (and perhaps did) materialize at Alex's shoulder.

Alex predictably jumped back, startled by the sudden company. I glared at the Sheyd for a moment—Alex didn't need more fire on the conflagration that was burning his perception of his place in the cosmos to the ground.

"And you aren't a person?" Alex asked, his lips pressed in a thin, furious line.

"I'm certainly a person. I'm not a human person, if that is what you mean," Isingway replied, sniffing as if offended that only humans might be considered people—and I supposed he had a point.

"Isingway is one of the Sheydim. His brother Oro, who goes by Oscar, works for APD, and he's gone missing."

Alex opened and closed his mouth a few times. I could see him processing not only the existence of Sheydim, which he had probably heard of only in passing—or if he had any knowledge, they were probably synonymous with demons—but also the fact that at least one of his fellow cops wasn't actually human.

"Oro was, is, a good man," Isingway pressed.

Alex looked between us. I wondered if he would demand to be involved now that he knew the victim was one of his people. I waited, trying to give Alex the time he needed to work through the new information, then he sighed.

"Well, if it is one of us," he said, "make sure you get him back in one piece, Ze'ev. We need all the good men we can get." He was forcing the attitude; I knew it, he knew it, I wondered if Isingway could sense that too. But it was a moot point as Alex shook my hand and then Isingway's, and headed off to his own car.

It wasn't that simple. I knew there would be a reckoning over this sooner or later, and I would have to come clean, not just about this but about the other dirt in the APD.

When Alex was gone, Isingway turned to me. "Did you learn anything? What did Basken tell you?"

"Nothing he meant to," I grinned, "but yeah, I think I know what's going on. I just need to do some research."

Chapter 8

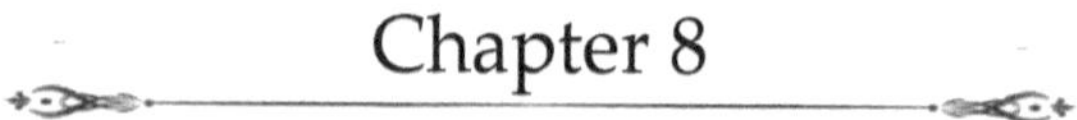

I didn't actually know what was going on, but Basken had given away more than he probably meant to. Namely, that Sheydim bodies could be broken down and used for spell components. It was a ghastly proposition, butchering a living man for his parts, but one I wouldn't put past anyone in Basken's circle. I dropped Isingway off back downtown near the Whole Foods. I didn't know where he was staying, but I didn't really want him with me anymore than absolutely necessary. Especially not when I headed to my workshop. Not that the Sheydim didn't know where that was. I had summoned one of them, a powerful one of them, to the lab when Peter Stübbe had kidnapped Sandy and left Rivkah a bloody mess.

Even now, months later, I was hesitant to open the door to the little warehouse Rivkah and I kept as a workshop and office. After all, Basken's cultists and

Stübbe had found it, the Sheydim definitely knew where it was, and I would be willing to put money down on Grin and his ghouls knowing about it too. I took a deep breath and pushed open the door, steeling myself to find my safe haven ransacked and my Rivkah, my assistant and friend, lying in a pool of blood. Of course, nothing was out of place. The books were on the shelves, the various occult knickknacks and components were all in place, and Rivkah was sitting at her desk staring into some scientific tool that I couldn't remember the function of, blasting some low-tempo terrifying music from speakers she had brought in.

As I came in, she turned and smiled before reaching over to turn her music down. Rivkah was an extremely attractive young woman, petite at 5'2" but extremely curvy. I had trained myself years ago to lock my eyes to her face to avoid looking down her shirt, which was a real danger as she tended to wear low cut band tees or tank tops. Luckily, today she paired it with a black lace cardigan, giving her some semblance of modesty. I never enforced a dress code; I always felt that if I was distracted by Rivkah's looks or body, that was entirely my problem and I needed to be a better human. Rivkah was goth as they come, heavy black eye makeup, black lipstick, black nails, purple and black hair, and just a smorgasbord of tattoos and piercings. But despite the death metal sex kitten look she carefully cultivated, Rivkah was both a nice Jewish girl and a brilliant scientist.

She had been working on her doctorate in chemical engineering when she had stumbled upon a malik intent on ruining her life. She could have probably continued with her life after the incident, but between the sudden realization that the world was so much larger and stranger than she had thought and the discovery that us mystics never bothered to apply modern scientific principles to magical study, she had decided that she needed to join the Beit Din. I don't know how she originally felt about becoming my "apprentice," but once we realized what she had actually wanted to achieve, we found a sort of harmony.

I let her research to her heart's content, and she helped me stay alive. I also had the unfortunate side task of dealing with Nathan and the associated paperwork that her purchases brought us. Eventually, I'm sure she would compile a report for the Beit Din several hundred pages long that detailed the scientific method behind the magic and mysticism we practiced; I only hoped it would be read and respected by her peers in the magical community.

I glanced at her bookshelf as I walked past. Books on maths, chemistry, biology, physics graced the shelves. But there were also books on alchemy and on the biochemistry of angels and the molecular nature of demons. Most of the books were new age nonsense, but within the pages and pages of weirdness, there would be grains of truth, or at least hypotheses that brought Rivkah closer to understanding the world we lived in.

"Yom tov, Rivkah," I greeted when I was close enough to be heard over her music without shouting.

"Hey, Ze'ev." She grinned at me, was it forced? I hoped she was still happy, I knew that the attack from the werewolf had left her more than a little shaken.

She said she didn't remember anything that happened after Stübbe attacked her until she woke up in the hospital. I was grateful to the Sheyd I had summoned, he must have stabilized her, watched over her until the ambulance arrived. What the medics must have thought about all the arcana around the shop was anyone's guess.

I stepped up to her to see what she was working on.

"What have you got going?"

She gave me a quick hug—making my blood pressure rise for a moment—before backing up a step to gesture at her desk. "I'm trying to figure out what's happening when you invoke an amulet or talisman."

"Angels," I said dismissively, earning me a mean look before her smile returned.

It was an old game. My answer may be flippant, but it was technically true, but it wasn't specifically what she was looking for. She wanted to know how or why the talisman was important, she wanted to know why it helped in the casting of spells or invocation.

"Yeah, okay, and why do they listen to you, of all people?"

"Why wouldn't they listen to me? What's not to listen to?" I protested with a grin before moving back over to my own work area. Unlike Rivkah's desk, which had all manner of scientific equipment on it, my own larger desk looked like it came off the set of a fantasy movie about an alchemist. Mortar and pestle, jeweler's wax, casting tools, notebooks filled with scrawled and annotated thoughts. But something was missing …

"Where are my manuscripts?" I asked.

I normally kept my oldest and most important books, scrolls, and manuscripts on a small shelf behind a glass door. They were likely worth a fortune to a collector, or a wing named in my honor to a museum, but they were real, real magical and holy texts. Seeing the shelves emptied of the manuscripts made my heart leap into my throat, and I felt dizzy.

"What? Ze'ev, we talked about this. I took them to Jordi to store correctly at the university," Rivkah said, raising one pierced eyebrow in concern over my apparent inability to remember basic things.

I vaguely remembered the conversation, and it made sense; after all, those texts were precious and delicate. The university had the facilities to keep them whole and safe, though I didn't actually trust any archeology or theology professors not to flip out and try to claim them for their own. Still, I had been planning on plumbing them for any references to the corporeal form of Sheydim being used. I doubted I would find anything. While the Sheydim were half spirit and were called demons, they were also half human, and using their internals externally would certainly be construed as murder and necromancy.

I slowly sank into my chair and considered my options. There was always the internet, the greatest boon to the investigator since the invention of the truth. I hummed the niggun I had been singing in Oro's apartment. The music was a comfort, even when overlaid by the haunting and guttural sounds coming from Rivkah's system. There were too many things going on; between the Ser'im, Sara, Isingway, and the damned vampire thing that Father Jerry made me fight, I was worn thin. I felt Rivkah's hand on my shoulder, and she squeezed, giving the tense muscle a bit of a massage. I dropped my chin to my chest, enjoying the bit of contact and ease of tightness.

"Did you need them for something?" Rivkah asked as she released her hold and dug an elbow into my shoulder—the pressure felt fantastic.

"Yeah, need to do some research, more Basken shit," I explained.

She pulled back and walked around me.

"Oliver Basken? The Necromancer?"

"The very same. I found some evidence of rituals, and I need to figure out what his stooges are up to. Whatever they're doing it can't be—"

I paused as my eyes fell on the safe I kept in one corner of the room. It contained books of sorcery and treif magic, dark manuscripts from insane men who sought to turn the world to their whims. I had used one of those books to summon a Sheyd when I needed to catch Stübbe. It had culminated with me making a deal for a man's life, traipsing through a Sheydim city, and coming face to face with one of the most powerful creatures in all of creation. But, if I needed to know about a cursed ritual, especially something that involved harvesting Sheydim body parts, where better to look?

I rose from my chair and walked to the safe, aware that Rivkah's dark brown eyes were on me.

"What are you doing?" she asked.

"Well, I'm pretty sure I've liberated some books on necromancy. If I can find out what their plan is, I might be able to stop it."

Rivkah followed after me. "Didn't you tell me that these books are strictly off limits? That just reading them could be corrupting, a sin, in and of themselves?"

I turned and glanced at her, more tattoos than a Japanese gangster and plenty of piercings. She was far from orthodox, but I knew what she was asking; she wanted to know where lines were drawn and why.

"Yeah, using any of them would be a very bad thing, but I need to use them to stop someone else from doing it. Look, I wouldn't ask you or Sandy or anyone else to do this. But I have to. I have to figure out what's going on before it's too late."

Rivkah looked skeptical at my explanation, but other than screwing up her pouty lips in disapproval, she didn't say anything else.

I squatted next to the safe and punched in the

fourteen digit code to open the door. Fourteen seemed excessive, but it was a number combination that was drilled into my head, something I would never forget, and it was something that no one else would guess. With a slight sigh, the safe opened.

I glanced back at Rivkah and gave her a pointed look, urging her to go back to her work. She returned my look with a worried glare and walked back to her desk. With what little privacy I now had, I perused the spines of the books in the shelf. They were in a variety of languages—German, Arabic, Latin, Spanish. I would love to be able to say I was fluent in all of those languages, but the truth was that beyond English, Yiddish, and Hebrew, I only spoke a bit of Spanish, enough to order my favorite food at the small taco trucks that dotted Austin. I reached out and touched the spines of the books. I knew what each of them was, I had gone through hell to get some of them. Butted heads with monsters, guardians, and, of course, had to haggle with books' previous owners to secure this collection of awful tomes on behalf of the abominable Mr. Grin.

I wasn't going to give them to Grin, that much was sure. Eventually, that would bring the two of us to blows, but I was hoping I could come up with a plan for putting an end to the homicidal supernatural hitman before that happened. But gathering the evil books and safeguarding them against the maniacs who would actually use them seemed like a good idea at the time.

Before I became one of those maniacs out of necessity. Now, here I was delving back into the cesspool of evil.

I grimaced as I pulled one of the German books and one of the English books out of the safe and took the two books back to my desk.

I flipped through the German book, *Buch der Kinder*. It was a leather-bound book, warm to the touch, it felt like it was moving under my fingers. Each page was vellum, and I had the painful realization that those pages of vellum were probably not calfskin. With a sigh, I turned the ghastly pages one by one, leaning on my knowledge of Yiddish to translate the German. Surprisingly enough, though, most of the text within was Hebrew, Aramaic, and Arabic. Ancient, nearly indecipherable to me, but not what I was expecting from a German titled book. The text squirmed in my vision, writhing into obscene shapes and horrifying truths that scratched at my brain through alien texts. For some reason, the book pulled my mind back to the Sheyd I had summoned, and Lillith herself.

I closed my eyes to block out the writhing words on the page, but I could hear them, a language that seemed older than time itself, with whispered pronouncements in the true language of creation. It made demands and promises. The book wanted me to read it, it demanded I let loose what was bound in the chains of ink written on the flesh-vellum under my fingers. It stung my skin where I made contact with the book, but it was pain that brought pleasure, a tinging venom that crept up my hands towards my heart. My muscles spasmed as the electric feeling of corruption washed out of *Buch der Kinder* and consumed me.

It reminded me of meeting Lillith in the City East-of-Nod, where she had killed me and frozen me in the moment of shattered, agonizing bliss. Remembering the Queen of Sheydim caused my loins to stir, even the memory of her, as terrifying as she was. I growled at my own weakness and crossed my legs. I needed to pay this favor to Isingway and extricate myself from the Sheydim entirely; they were too strange, too powerful, and too terrifying for me to keep being involved in their affairs.

I closed the terrifying leather-bound book and slid it away from me. I didn't really want to even touch it more than I had to. I pulled my eyes away from it and focused instead on the English book. Instead of an upsetting supple leather cover, this book seemed bound in cloth-covered planks of thin wood. It looked earthy, more humble and less menacing than the *Buch der Kinder*. I gingerly brushed the corner of the book with my fingertips but felt nothing sinister.

Despite the stark contrast in how the books looked and felt, I knew that judging the second by the first would be a terrible mistake. I lifted the clothbound book and turned it in my hands. There were no indications on the outside about what the interior held, but I had attained this book in a crypt found through a star map and guarded by something that I feared had once been human. I was sure it was, in fact, the last surviving copy of An *Account of the Magical Uses of Corpses*. Maybe the title sounded better in Olde English.

It was a bit on the nose for what I was looking for, and my eyes drifted back to the *Buch der Kinder*. Why had I even grabbed that? I could still feel it when I glanced in its direction, calling me. Had it influenced me to grab it from the safe? I rose and grabbed a hand towel from my desk; wrapping it around the corner of the leather book, I took it back to the safe and reshelved it.

Immediately, I felt better. I breathed a sigh of relief and sat back at my desk to look through an ancient book of necromancy. It was still an awful thing to read, the archaic English the book was written in was barely decipherable. I crawled through the text, turning each page slowly as I tried to determine what I was looking at, and really what I was even looking for. The reality of the situation was that references to using demonic, faerie, or spirit blood and organs to work dark magic could mean anything. And it could be listed in the contents of the spellwork or in the margins or maybe in an off-hand passage. It was like looking through a haystack that someone had lit on fire while looking for a piece of hay that someone had painted off-yellow.

But I didn't have any better leads, so I continued to pour over the text. I wished I could put it down, go relax for bit, maybe plan a lesson for Sandy that wasn't as gruesome as hunting and killing monsters. But with Isingway's brother missing, it meant that I could have an extremely limited amount of time before things went from bad to worse. If Oro hadn't already been dissected for whatever sickening spell work was intended.

Time ticked away as the disgusting words and suggestions in the book slithered through my mind. It felt like emails that had pushed their way through toxic sludge were slowly doing donuts in my brain. But none of the spell work in the book was enticing to me, so that was a plus. I turned the page. Even my body felt heavy and lethargic. I thought about giving up when I noticed something odd. This last page I had turned was laying differently than all the others; it wasn't flush.

I turned the page back over and looked closely at the spine. There, cut so close as to almost be invisible without careful inspection, was the remnants of a page that had been torn, or rather, meticulously cut from the book. A missing page. Of course, this book was old, ancient even; the idea that someone had at some point desecrated a foul book on stealing power from the dead was not very outlandish.

I considered the various means I might use to discover what had happened to the page. I could dream walk or use some method to tap into the very memory of the book itself, though that had risks. This was an evil thing, wielded by evil men and women throughout its sordid history. I wasn't sure I would like to see any of that. I leaned in close, studying the cut, when a peculiar scent hit my nostrils. It was ash, ashes and tobacco and … decay. I brushed my hand along the page and held my palm up to the light. Stuck to my skin were flecks of ash with the slightest green tint.

I didn't need to dive into the book's past, the green necrotic tobacco was enough to tell me exactly who had stolen the missing page from the tome. The question was how did I confront the King of Ghouls's hitman?

Chapter 9

At some point during my research, pointless reading when the answer had actually been a missing page, Rivkah had left. While I was putting away the books, locking them back into the safe, and organizing things, I heard her coming back in. And with her, I heard the chattering of a teenage girl. Sandy was here. I frowned at the presence of both of my apprentices. I hadn't made a plan for teaching Sandy today. I enjoyed teaching and lecturing, I hated planning.

"Hey, Ze'ev!" Sandy called.

I stood and waved at her and Rivkah, dusting off my knees with my other hand.

"Find what you were looking for?" Rivkah asked.

I offered her a grimace and a waving hand as if to say more or less. "I found where to look next, no pleasant answers."

"Ooh," Sandy whispered, her eyes going big with

excitement. "What are we hunting?"

When I had first met the precocious blond teen, she had acted disinterested and aloof. Even when she moved to Austin to study with me and Rivkah, much to my chagrin, she had mostly seemed nervous and timid. She had caught the attention of Sheydim and lived her life looking over her shoulder at shadows. Now, after a few months, a kidnapping, and a life-or-death fight against a werewolf, she was much more courageous. Maybe too much so. I was hoping to send her down the path of the scholar, or maybe the exorcist. Doing it all and adding monster hunter to that list was a recipe for disaster.

It made you live a life of lies, danger, and pain. I didn't want that for her. But she seemed damned and determined to discover all of the most exciting ways to die. I studied her face for a moment; she was so young and innocent. But she already had more experience with the supranatural and spirits than most people would ever run against in their lifetimes. I imagined her older, with scars like mine, a jaded weariness that comes from living a life one night at a time. I imagined her lying to her future boyfriends or girlfriends about where she was at night, about the inner pain that would bring. I also tried to imagine her sitting at a desk and working a 9-5. Despite my best effort, I couldn't.

"We're not hunting anything," I admonished. "I, on the other hand, am hunting a ghoul."

"What? Why wouldn't I be coming with you?" Sandy

asked.

"Why would you come with me?" I countered. "It's a dangerous thing. Ghouls aren't dybbukim. They aren't looking for healing, they aren't part of being an exorcist."

"I would come with you because you're supposed to be teaching me about this stuff!" she argued.

I saw Rivkah raise an eyebrow behind Sandy. I knew what she was thinking. We had talked about the future with Sandy and how we would direct her learning. We had also discussed the fact that Sandy wanted to hunt monsters and how quickly that would get her killed.

"Well, I'm not going anywhere at the moment. You're forgetting the first part of looking for anything, hunting, or healing is research." I grinned at her groan. "So, let's have a seat, and I can tell you all about ghouls." Sandy nodded and tossed her backpack in a corner before going to grab a chair. I frowned, seeing Rivkah drag her own chair over. "What are you doing?"

"Lecture time. You never taught me about monsters," she said with a grin. "Besides, you don't lecture me on stuff anymore; I miss professor Kaplan sometimes."

I rolled my eyes. "You miss being a career student," I corrected.

"Maybe, so just let me enjoy the rare opportunities." She grinned as she plopped down. Of course, she was sort of joking. While I didn't give her too many lectures or lessons these days, seeing as she was way smarter than I could ever hope to be, I knew that she attended lectures and symposiums any chance she got. Then again, all of that was theory and supposition, I had real world experience to share.

"Okay, fine," I said as Sandy finally sat down, notebook in hand to take notes. "Class is in session."

Despite my objections, I actually loved times when I could just get up in front of someone and teach. It meant I could just talk and chat. Outside of classroom settings, or whatever this counted as, I didn't get that many opportunities to discuss these topics at length. Even with Rivkah, she was more interested in the science, and she was so far out of my league intellectually speaking that she should be leading any discussion. But supernatural and cryptozoological creatures? That was my forte.

"Ghouls are an ancient race. The word itself is Arabic and originates in pre-Islamic Arabic cultures, though I assume the ghouls are even older than that. This is one case in which the folklore has hardly changed at all. Ghouls were said to inhabit graveyards and catacombs and feast on human remains. I think most scholars would assume that ghouls were desert scavengers that had mange. And ghouls do have certain animal-like traits; they look like a hybrid of human, hyena. You've actually seen them before. They accompanied Stübbe during that whole … thing."

I saw Sandy stiffen but shook my head.

"Most the time, though, ghouls operate alone. They can be pack creatures, but only if they have a strong enough leader; generally, you'll never see more than one at a time. They're gangly, feral creatures. And most humans would call them monsters."

"You wouldn't?" Rivkah asked with a raised eyebrow, the fluorescent light above glinting off her eyebrow ring.

"Well, the word monster is problematic, right?" I answered. "Ghouls are intelligent, conscious, not only sentient but capable of conversation and reason." I paused, seeing Rivkah's judgmental look continue. "I know, I know; I in particular have a bit of a history with ghouls, but we'll get to that in a moment.

"I don't know where ghouls came from, or rather, how they came to be. Obviously, our earliest records and knowledge of them comes from the Middle East, but at this time, there are ghouls all around the world. Anywhere humans live, you can find them as well. But the most famous ghouls still come from that point of origin."

"Famous ghouls? Do they pose as humans?" Sandy asked, enamored by the idea that a celebrity was actually some secret supernatural creature.

"No, I don't think they could, not unless they are in extremely low light and no one gets close enough," I explained. "No, I mean legendary ghouls. Specifically, Ghul-al-Biyaban and Baalrachius. Now, Ghul-al-

Biyaban probably isn't the creature's name but a title. It essentially translates to the ghoul of Biyaban, or of the desolate place. For all we know, Baalrachius and al-Biyaban may be the same person … thing … ghoul," I finished lamely.

"Okay," Sandy said slowly, disappointed. "But what is a ghoul? I mean, all they do is eat dead bodies. Are they really something you need to worry about?"

"Am I not getting there? You interrupt and then wonder why it takes me so long!" I shook my head in mock outrage. "Look, for a very long time, Jews, and not just Jews but Christians, Muslims, and plenty of other faiths, believed that people's bodies would be taken to heaven; and in many cultures, dead bodies were seen to be unclean or corrupting. So, we have not only creatures that were inhuman and terrifying to look at, but they were engaging in disgusting behavior that most people at the time found to be not only morally and sanitarily disgusting but spiritually blasphemous."

I paused and looked at the women's faces. Sandy's eyes were huge, she still had a fascination with the way the supernatural world works. Rivkah was waiting for details, she wanted to know the science behind these things.

"One fascinating aspect of the supernatural world, the monsters and demons and creatures, is how adept they are at cleaning up after themselves. It's why cryptids are cryptids and things like ghouls are legends and not common knowledge. Let's say something dies, something like a wyvern. It's big, it's dangerous, it can fly; why doesn't anyone know they exist?"

"It's a government conspiracy?" Sandy shouted, making Rivkah laugh out loud.

"Just like the lack of good delis?" Rivkah asked innocently.

"Or how awful most 'kosher' pickles are?" Sandy rejoined.

They kept going, naming off various petty annoyances before bursting into a fit of giggles. I had obviously missed some inside joke between the two women.

"Uh, well no," I said when they finally calmed down. "At least not our government. Intelligent non-humans, like Sheydim, ghouls, and other entities, take great care to hide their existence from humanity. So, they swoop in, clean up the dead, mislead humans from finding the real answer. That, and people like us, you and me, cover up the truth as well."

"Why?" Sandy asked, and Rivkah gave me a pointed look. I had never answered Rivkah when she asked the same question.

I sat down on the edge of my desk and crossed my arms, trying to put what I was thinking into words.

"Because knowing sucks. Imagine spending every night wondering if an alukah will be smashing through your window to steal your soul, or if you meet someone new and wonder if they are secretly a Sheydim." I shrugged. "Because knowing is terrifying but also beautiful, the world of magic is awesome and awful all at once." I paused and met Rivkah's eyes. "Because most of us aren't scientists, most of us are scared and xenophobic. Most people can't handle Jews thinking differently than them, and we have been hunted down and attacked, accused of being in league with spirits and demons." I stood up and paced a moment, trying to calm down.

"Because at the end of the day, humans are the most dangerous and cruelest monsters on this planet, and the only thing knowing about the greater world would accomplish is giving those monsters more tools for cruelty and more victims to use them on."

We sat there in silence for several minutes. They were swallowing the harsh statement; I was reflecting on my own part in what amounted to a secret Cold War. Which side was I on? If I was on humanity's side, then why didn't I spend all my time hunting monsters, or expose monsters to the government, let humanity panic for a bit and then wipe out the threat, which it certainly would do. If I was on the side of protecting the supernatural from humanity's capricious and cruel nature, then why did I hunt down the monsters that fed on humanity?

Like most everything, things were painted in shades of gray, blending the dark and the light, humanity and the supernatural. Like the Sheydim themselves, shadows and light, good and bad. All things existed in a dichotomy of circumstances and learned behaviors. What behaviors was I teaching Sandy now? If I continued to only teach her the science and meditation, if I only gave her tools for study and being a scholar, would she go and get herself killed because I never taught her to be a warrior?

"So … are there diplomats?" Sandy's question broke my concentration, and I stared at her, trying to figure out what she meant. Luckily, she continued. "Like, are there people who try to work with the supernatural communities to uphold treaties and keep people safe?"

I considered the question. "There probably are in other religions or groups. For the Beit Din, no, or at least not officially. I used to have a truce of sort with the ghouls in Texas, but that's fallen apart. Basically, it's up to each hunter or exorcist to manage the relationship between humankind and the super- or supernatural in their area. HQ doesn't love it, but it stays out of it for the most part."

Sandy looked dissatisfied with my answer, which was worrisome. Would she head to the nearest graveyard and attempt to open an embassy?

"They also police themselves. Remember, a lot of them, like the Sheydim, are intelligent, they have their own governments and organizations. So while there aren't official treaties or anything like that, there are essentially invisible social contracts between the various groups to keep things from slipping into chaos."

"Okay, so if ghouls aren't just mindless monsters that need hunting, why are we hunting one?" Rivkah asked, bringing the conversation back to the original topic.

"We aren't, I am. But it's because I've been asked to find someone, a Sheyd, and I think the ghoul is connected to his disappearance."

Rivkah stood up, bouncing as she rose. "What? Damnit, Ze'ev, you didn't say anything about that; you said it was related to Basken!"

"Basken? That cult leader?" Sandy cut in.

I shot Rivkah a glare; Sandy wasn't ready to know the true depths of human evil.

"Yeah, the same one; and yes, Rivkah, it is," I raised a hand to stop Rivkah from interrupting me, "but I think it involves Grin. I'm sure it does, which means that it's way too dangerous for Sandy or you to be involved."

"And how does not involving me usually go, Ze'ev? Did you remember to submit my hospital bills to the Beit Din?" Her question was pointed and cutting. When I tried to take Basken down alone, I had nearly been killed; and when I did the same for Stübbe, Sandy was kidnapped and Rivkah hospitalized.

I threw my arms in the air. "I know, I know. But there's not much choice. I try to keep you out of harm's way, and then these things come after me and they come after you. But do you think it would be safer next to me? Where you're directly in the line of fire?" I turned to Sandy. "Because that's what being a monster hunter means, Sandy, it means you are always in the line of fire and the stray shots are likely going to hit your friends and family. It means that every time I build a relationship with someone who *isn't* in this world that I'm building that relationship on a lie that could get them killed. And I don't want that life for you. I don't want that life for anyone …" I trailed off and sighed, putting my face in my hands and rubbing my eyes.

I considered telling the two of them about my encounter at the zoo. It made things more dangerous, made them even more likely to be collateral damage, especially if they were with me. But I knew that if I told Sandy about the Ser'im, she would want to know everything. And if I mentioned them to Rivkah, she would demand to come with me to "watch my back." I didn't need either of those things to happen at the moment. I needed them to …

"Trust me," I said. "I know what I'm doing, and I'm not in over my head, not yet."

A lie, not even a particularly good one, but the best one I could muster at the moment.

"By and large, though, I don't spend most of my time hunting, or at least I didn't until recently. Most of my life, this job was about dealing with dybbukim and the occasional supernatural occurrence. Or helping other people with cryptids. I've fought off more chupacabra than I have anything from our own tradition. Even then, most of them were coyotes with mange." I smiled a little.

"What changed?" Sandy asked. I looked at her blankly, and she explained the question. "What changed from before when you hardly hunted, why are you doing it more now?"

"Well…I don't know, honestly," I answered. "Basken seemed to change things. See, that's the real problem, Sandy, people suck. People who tap into unclean or dark magic suck the worst of all. So, I had to go head-to-head with Basken and then Stübbe, who, while we call him a werewolf, was probably just an overpowered shapeshifting warlock."

"So you've been hunting people and not monsters?"

"People can be monsters just as much if not more so than any supernatural entity," I said plainly. "Like that dybbuk that was in your bathroom."

Sandy shifted uncomfortably, remembering how we had met, the inciting incident that had led to her training under me. "I remember."

"Right, you remember I was trying to comfort him, trying to help. It wasn't until he went violent and aggressive that I resorted to more forceful exorcism tactics."

"Yeah," she confirmed hesitantly, obviously unsure where I was going with this.

"Well, the reason that dybbuk turned nasty is because it had been summoned by someone nasty, Basken or someone in his cult. See, we live in something of a harmony in the world, and we as hunters and exorcists don't actually hunt monsters, what we hunt is disharmony. We seek out places and ways in which the natural equilibrium of the world has been thrown off and we address that. In the Beit Din, we look for those discordant moments within or surrounding the Jewish community, but all of us essentially perform the same role." I finished my big speech and turned back to face the two women.

Rivkah looked thoughtful, hopefully thinking about our task and the nature of the world in a new light. I was proud of that little speech. I don't know that it was completely accurate, but in the early mornings sitting in my car, waiting to face down some ghoul or Malik threat, this was what I had come up with. Sandy did not look impressed, she looked freaked out.

"Uh, Sandy, are you okay?" I asked.

"Are you saying that the old creepy ghost in my bathroom was an attack? On me? By a serial killer satanist?" Each part of her questions raised in pitch and volume.

Rivkah no longer looked thoughtful, she looked annoyed with me.

"Okay, no, not, well yes, a little, but not on purpose. I think that the dybbuk was brought over or displaced because of other things that Basken's group was doing, not a direct purposeful attack on you or your family. And Basken isn't a Satanist; most Satanists are atheists and frankly lovely people. Basken was a necromancer, the only thing he worships is power."

Sandy did not look comforted. I glanced at Rivkah, hoping she could help somehow. She looked back at me and shrugged before turning to Sandy.

"Girlfriend, what are you scared of? You've gone

head-to-head with crazy stuff, you've had brushes with dybbukim, Sheydim, werewolves, and ghouls! More than almost anyone on Earth other than psychos like Ze'ev, certainly more than any other teenage girl. You're a badass."

Sandy seemed to relax a little, blushing at the praise Rivkah heaped on her. I mouthed the words *thank you* to Rivkah and turned to grab a book from my non-cursed book shelf.

"Okay, so what makes a ghoul tick?" I asked as I resumed the lesson.

Chapter 10

After my lesson to the women, it was time to actually get to work. I needed to find a powerful and deadly ghoul, one who had already threatened to kill not only me but my friends and family as well. Last time I encountered Grin, he had found me. I had killed a ghoul, revealing myself and then waiting for the enforcer to hunt me down. How did I go about hunting him down? I didn't even know if he was in Texas.

I didn't want to go out and hurt ghouls. As much as I had beef with the creatures, and as disgusting as they were, they were living, sentient beings. But maybe I didn't have to hurt anyone; really, I just needed one to deliver a message. Despite the fact that I had been hunted and had things targeting me for a while now, I was still a hunter myself. I didn't need to rely on my bad luck to do my job for me.

I gathered a few tools from the workshop and headed

out into the city.

Before our falling out, I had actually had a contact in the Ghoul community, Shalnacht. Shalnacht was a ghoul that I could normally find in San Marcos. He had been something of an informer, aware of goings on in the supernatural world and monstrous community, if you could call it that. But last time I had dealt with him, he had betrayed me to Baalrachius, the King of Ghouls. He had been responsible for selling me out, getting me kidnapped, and really for getting me mixed up with Grin in the first place.

But he was also the ghoul I was most familiar with, one whose habits I knew. That meant that he would be the easiest to find.

I drove out to the San Marcos cemetery. Living in Texas, you got used to hot days and nights. It was hardly even cool, let alone cold. The evening air was pleasant, though, in the high 70s. And I had to admit that the state was beautiful. San Marcos rested along the San Marcos River—part of the Guadalupe watershed and river system, which ran from Kerrville to the Gulf— and through the years had maintained that riverside town feeling. Despite the sprawling college campus at the heart of the town, San Marcos had stayed quaint.

I got out of the car and stood next to it for several minutes, enjoying the quiet and clean air. *Maybe I should move somewhere less action-packed, somewhere where I could live a slower life.* But that was a pipe dream. The smaller towns in Texas didn't have much of a Jewish population, and despite my sometimes isolationist attitude, I needed the community around me to be happy. And so long as I was around the Jewish community, I would be called on to protect it.

That wasn't what I was doing now, though. I wasn't even protecting myself. I was endangering myself by sticking my neck out for the ghouls to tear off at their leisure. I began walking up towards the small tombs, family mausoleums, which is where I would find evidence of ghouls, or at the least their tunnels. I had a rocky history with the ghouls. I had told Sandy that our truce had fallen apart, but the truth was that what had happened had been close to an all-out war. Ghouls despised necromancers, and Basken riled them up enough that the ghouls wanted to kill any and all magic users. I was an enemy of the state, with my death ordered by Baalrachius himself.

But it was more than just that fight between Basken and the ghouls; ghouls had been with Stübbe too, when I caught up with him to rescue Sandy. Why had they been there? At the time, I had been too busy, too focused on survival and the fight to think about it. But now, as I walked back into the jaws of my flesh-eating enemies, I had to wonder … why had ghouls been with Stübbe? He had been a child-murdering monster, possibly a magic user himself. Something else floated up to my mind. Stübbe had mentioned that some woman had basically hired him to kill me. Basken had also mentioned a woman. And the Ser'im had mentioned the woman in the statue, that terrible entity that had killed the young woman just to fuck with me. Was that woman the same person? Was this all the same woman?

My blood ran cold, my stomach sinking into my pelvis as I remembered the three instances. Who was "she?" I had dismissed Basken as a basket case, a delusional madman, but Stübbe wasn't crazy, at least not in the same delusional way. Was it the same woman? Who had I made angry enough in the supernatural world to want to kill me? There were plenty of entities and people I had pissed off over the course of my career, but most of them weren't human enough to make plans, and those that were human enough were mostly men. I thought about the course of my life, the monsters, the people, the pain. I honestly couldn't think of anyone who would want me dead enough to enlist necromancers and ancient werewolves.

My hand hovered over the handle to the tomb where I had last seen Shalnacht. Maybe my paranoia was getting the better of me. But I had cause to be paranoid; too many people had tried to kill me recently to ignore, and I was heading right towards one of those *people* now. I took a moment to breathe, calming myself and bringing my mind back to center. Whatever else was going on, I needed to figure out what Grin was up to, and probably stop him. One step at a time, only the present moment, hineni.

With a small amount of clarity in purpose, I pulled open the door to the crypt and peered inside. No feral ghoul was waiting for me. The smell of dry rot and old dust hit my nose—it wasn't foul or gross, it just smelled like claustrophobia and dirt. I stepped in, flipping the flashlight on my phone on, and walked past the ornate stone angel that took up the middle of the room. There in the back was a hole. I didn't know if ghouls closed these off regularly, if they hid their tunnels, or if Shalnacht had just grown overconfident and placid in his self-preservation. Whatever the case, this was what I was looking for.

I could crawl into this hole and try to find the ghoul in his natural habitat, but from what little I understood, the creatures had a vast network of tunnels, and there was no guarantee that I would be able to find Shalnacht or wouldn't find myself going up against large number of the creatures. The other issue, of course, was that ghoul physiology was different than that of humans. There was a real possibility that traversing the tunnel would require contortions I was incapable of.

Luckily, I didn't need to dive into the disturbed earth and hunt through miles of tunnels to find what I was looking for. I sat with my back to the wall and scooped up a handful of dirt from the edge of the tunnel. I settled my gaze on the handful of soil and let my eyes lose focus. I breathed slowly, counting to ten with each inhale and exhale. Listening to the still quietness in the crypt, I could hear my pulse, my breath, the small shifts I made. All of the sounds that were normally hidden under the noise of life and living.

There was something sweet about the stillness in the crypt, it brought to mind the phrase *eternal rest*. It was peaceful. I pulled my mind back to my breathing. Some considered the point of meditation to empty your mind, but the truth is that's impossible to do. Instead, my goal was to focus the mind, force it to be mindful and in the moment. Force it to concentrate on the task at hand. I took in a lungful of air and blew the dirt from my hand. It created a cloud of dust in front of me, suspending in air as though frozen in time. I stood, maintaining my attention to my breath, forcing my thoughts on the inhale and exhale. I reached forward and carved a word in the dust by dragging my finger through the suspended particulate.

On my exhale, I intoned a prayer, a spell that would empower the word *tsud*, to hunt. The empty space where I had written the word pulsed with subtle power, awakening with my whispered prayers. I pictured a ghoul in my mind, imagining the way they looked and moved. I built as close a mental image of my prey as possible before pushing that image into the incantation. Without looking away from the slightly glowing cloud of dust, I flicked my flashlight app off.

The light from my spell pulsed gently and slowly formed an image. I could see the shape of a ghoul in the dust, formed of swirling illuminated particulate. It was rough, undefined, but the stretched-out form and unnatural movements left little doubt that I had found a target in my sights. I leaned forward and breathed in the glowing dust, sucking it into my lungs. The air and dust, pregnant with knowledge, infused me. I knew where my quarry was.

It would be difficult to put into words. I couldn't say where the ghoul was, I couldn't say how I knew. It was like the knowledge was baked in. The way my mother knew how to cook, she just did it. It was muscle memory and instinct and forgotten memories that took over. And just like a bubbie making the best matzo ball soup, I operated now on instinct. I pushed out of the crypt and walked through the cemetery. He knew I was there, I could feel that. But he wasn't running. He either thought I wasn't a threat or thought that I wouldn't find him. Both assumptions were wrong, but I was happy he was underestimating me. That would make my job easier.

I walked between the grave plots, letting my body carry me forward with no clear direction in mind. I knew where to go without knowing. And after a few moments, I found myself outside a newer crypt. Shalnacht was inside. He felt safe, he felt at home; I could feel it radiating off him from outside. I breathed deep, letting the spell I had used to locate the ghoul dissipate. I could use another spell to bind him, capture him before I entered, but that had some risks.

Witnesses were always a concern. I looked around and confirmed I was alone.

I reared back and kicked the door to the crypt open. In the darkness, there was a surprised yelp, and I used that sound to target as I surged forward. Shalnacht could see me, his night vision perfectly suited to the blackness inside the tomb, but I wasn't giving him time to react. Before he could scamper to his little hidey-hole, I tackled the ghoul and slammed him against the wall. We wrestled for a moment, but I pinned his arms to avoid his claws and jammed my knee against his chest, pressing my weight down.

My face was close enough to his that I could smell the reek of decay on his breath and hear the moisture of his swallows. I needed to be careful that he didn't lunge forward and bite, but I could feel him giving up. He was afraid now. Good.

"Howdy, Shalnacht; been a while."

The ghoul thrashed against me again, but it was half-hearted. He knew he was bested, and Shalnacht was a coward at heart. "I had no choice, Wolf, I had no choice. My king demands, I bow to my king. There is nothing else for I to do."

"Shh," I reprimanded gently. "Your king isn't here. I am. You're alone with me right now." Shalnacht let out a little whimper. "I'm going to stand. If you try to run or try to attack me, you will be dead before the thought finishes crossing your mind. I have cursed you and you cannot harm me." It was a bluff, but I knew Shalnacht didn't have any magical knowledge—for all he knew, I was being sincere.

I let go of his arms and stood, taking a few steps back, letting him clamber to his feet, though he stayed huddled over, breathing shallowly, casting trembling and furtive looks in my direction. That was fine. Him having a healthy fear of me would work in my favor; I didn't need him to like me.

"I'm looking for someone higher up in the food chain than you, Shalnacht. I'm looking for Grin."

The ghoul blinked its huge dark eyes at me, his snoutish face crinkling in what looked like a snarl, and he began making choking sounds. It took me a moment to realize he was laughing.

"Something funny?" I asked, though I already knew what the answer would be.

"You don't find Mr. Grin, Mr. Grin finds you. And when he does, it won't matter what curses you have, it doesn't matter what power. He will eat you; he will taste your bones, and your flesh, and your dying breath."

"You should hope not, Shalnacht." I grinned at him. I wasn't really good at being sinister, but I was decent at being gruff. I hoped the two would work interchangeably. "That curse connects us. He kills me, your skull goes pop. My dying breath gets sucked into Grin's gob and the next thing the world knows is what the inside of your head looks like." The threat was completely empty, but I knew he wouldn't risk it.

When I had gone head-to-head with Grin before, while apprehending Basken, I had bluffed him into thinking I had a powerful magical ward that would keep him away. Grin had fallen for my bluff and retreated, which meant he had no idea what I was actually capable of or how spells worked. It also hinted at him not being able to even sense magic energies. At the end of the day, it gave me an entire blindside in ghouls to take advantage of. Most creatures were either magical or capable of using magic, not both, with the Sheydim being an exception to that rule.

Shalnacht looked terrified, his long claws scritching at his scalp as though he was searching for a way to find and excise the magic I claimed was digging into his brain. I let him dig, keeping my eyes locked on his.

"How do you think I found you, Shalnacht? Did you think it was a coincidence? I've known where you were since you first betrayed me; I've had my spells threaded deep into your flesh. Now, are you going to do what I ask, or are you going to shuffle off this mortal coil?"

My question hung in the air, Shalnacht probably weighing how terrible a death Mr. Grin would visit on him against the one I was promising. I hoped that was what he was doing anyway. If he was somehow sniffing out my lies, it could be game over, and I would have to just fight Shalnacht hand to hand. I knew I could win that little scuffle, but I might not make it out uninjured, and I would be back at square one.

Finally, he answered me. "I don't know where find Grin," he admitted.

"Then you better start looking. When you find him, tell him I'm looking for him, waiting for him. Spread it through your network contacts if you need to. If I don't hear from Mr. Grin within the next three days, make sure you've said your final goodbyes."

Shalnacht whimpered and hung his head. I didn't feel guilty. Last time I had spoken to him, trying to track down Basken, this awful monster had delivered me into the claws of Baalrachius and Grin himself. As far as I was concerned, he owed me, and if threatening him was the only way to get that karmic debt repaid and repay my own debt to the Sheydim, then so be it.

I turned away from the ghoul, trusting my threat of linked life to keep him from attacking me, and left the crypt. Now I could return to Austin and try to prepare for my coming guest.

Chapter 11

You know things are dire when I'm considering heading to Crisp and calling on Domah. It wasn't that I didn't like the angel, quite the contrary, I owed him almost all of my magical knowledge and understanding. I loved the angel like family. But he was painful to be around, the memories I had in that barn were traumatic. Not in the personal tragedy sort of way but in the *human minds were not built to perceive such things* way. It was more than that, though; Domah's mere presence hurt. He was an angel, a being so powerful that his mere existence dwarfed my mortal life. Even short encounters with the angel could lead to months of nightmares, which was something I actively tried to avoid.

But I was embroiled in some heavy hitters now — Mr. Grin, Sheydim, whoever "she" was. It wouldn't be bad to have a heavy hitter in my corner. I could drag

Sandy up north with me. Really, if she wanted to be a hunter, knowing and training under Domah like I had was her best bet for survival. But like I said, encounters with Domah couldn't be taken lightly, and there was a certain innocence lost when you encountered beings like that. I didn't know that I could be the catalyst for that loss; I still hoped I could dissuade her from hunting all together. But what if I couldn't? What if I kept tools away from her and she ended up getting killed because I was being overly cautious, or because I was trying to make decisions for her?

There was also Anthony I had to consider. I didn't need to train him into a hunter or fighter, but I had promised to figure out the nature of his abilities. And so long as I didn't involve Domah, I couldn't honestly say I was using every tool in my arsenal to answer that question. But there were other concerns there. What if Anthony was descended from something demonic, not of this reality? Or what if he were the distant offspring of Nephilim? There were a thousand things Anthony could be, from a hundred different cultures around the world. Would Domah be obligated to destroy Anthony if they met? Would I be endangering the kid? Or was I simply holding off from an answer that would grant him some kind of peace and self-acceptance?

There were no easy answers. I stopped at Dan's in Buda to grab a burger and ate it in the car as I drove, considering the dilemma of the teenagers and the angel. It boiled down to me making decisions for others. Did

I have the right to do that? The simple answer to that was: of course I did. I was privy to information that most people simply didn't have access to, or wouldn't believe even if they did. That put me in the frustrating position of being like a parent to a curious child. Every day, some unknowing innocent would put their hand on the stove of the supernatural world, and I would need to stop them without letting them know why. I didn't just have the right to make decisions for others, I had the obligation to.

But did that carry over to Domah and the kids? I felt like that was a tougher decision to make. There were so many factors to consider when you were dealing with the supernatural. Factors that could lead to death, corruption, or insanity. Kabbalistic writings were filled with warnings and allegory about men losing their minds while attempting to discern the secrets of the universe. And that was a fair warning too. People did lose their minds, and not just people who went too hard on psychedelic drugs chasing visions and prophecies promised by things that lived between the veils of various realities. People who saw too much too quickly, people who encountered things that were not or empty spaces filled with the unquiet rage of the unrepentant dead.

At the end of the drive, as I pulled into the parking lot for my little workshop, I decided to leave Domah out of this for now. Introducing a couple of kids to an angel because I was getting nervous about the bed I had made sounded shitty to me. That was the other side of things. Second guessing the self. I was a big proponent of acting on gut instinct. Sometimes going quick and not overthinking things could be the difference between life and death. I almost preferred the near-death, no-time-to-think style of decision making to one where I had to sit and weigh all the possibilities. Maybe that was an attempt to avoid responsibility.

With those self damning thoughts, I started to get out of my car when my phone went off. No rest for the mildly wicked, I supposed. It was Father Mankowitz. Frowning, I pulled myself out of the car and walked towards the door of my workshop while answering. "Hey, Jerry."

"Hey there, Wolf, you got a minute?" The voice on the other side sounded tired, worn down. That wasn't necessarily a surprise; he was a hunter, we were always run down and tired.

"Yeah, sure, Jerry. What's up?" I asked, pushing through the door and waving at Rivkah and Sandy.

"A couple of things. First, the diocese here got word from Rome that there's, well, we call 'em 'loose prophets.' But it's someone who experiences prophecies or can see things others can't ..." he trailed off.

"You're describing half of the supernatural world and more than half of the hunter and exorcist community, Jerry." I smirked.

"Yeah, but these are different. They're cursed, or not cursed, but they're touched, followed by bad luck, tend to get the raw end of the deal and can lead to danger for others. Anyway, there's supposedly one of these in Austin, and we're looking for them. Would you keep an eye open for it?"

"It?" I asked, disliking the word used for a human being. My mind immediately turned towards Anthony. He was Catholic, and he certainly had visions. He had also had an extremely hard life in the foster care system. A good kid, though, a good person.

"Them," Jerry corrected himself, a tad too late.

"Uh. Okay, yeah, I'll keep an eye out. You said there was something else?" I asked, eager to move on. I certainly wouldn't be turning Anthony over to the Catholic church anytime soon.

"Well, you remember our friend from the church?" he asked hesitantly. I rolled my eyes—was he about to try to chastise me again about the Sheyd? "Well, like I said, we keep track of them, how powerful they're getting, movements, all of that. And I think that there's a vampire in Austin, it looks to be hunting too."

"You think there's a vampire here?" I asked, a little bewildered. I was also confused as to why he was telling me; vampires, at least his flavor of vampires, were firmly in his camp's list of duties. "Okay ... are you asking for a couch to crash on, or what? What's going on?"

"No, I, I think it's hunting you, Ze'ev."

His statement hung in the air for several minutes. I must have made a face because Sandy and Rivkah were staring at me. That or they had heard me say the V-word.

"Excuse me, Jerry? Did you just say that a vampire that you asked me to help kill has decided to track me down and hunt me because I helped you?" I asked.

It was Jerry's turn to be silent. I could almost feel his shame through the phone.

"I know, I know, it's not usually how these things operate."

"Don't they? Jerry? Don't they?" I shouted back at him. "Because every shitty possession movie I've ever seen has the demon latching on to everyone involved."

"Hey, man, I said I'm sorry!" Jerry growled back.

"No, actually, you fucking didn't," I hissed through my teeth. I wasn't about to let him act like I was the bad guy here. He was silent for a moment, probably getting control of his own anger.

"Look, I'll come down there and—"

"Don't bother. Just tell me where it was seen or sensed or whatever you people do. I'll take care of it," I snapped.

Jerry kept protesting for a few minutes but eventually spilled the details. I growled a little—not on purpose, just in irritation—as I hung up and moved to my desk to grab a few tools of the trade. I didn't know much about the demon that created vampires, but I had seen how Jerry dispatched it. And I knew more than a little about exorcising intruding things. Jerry claimed the vampire couldn't be saved, that the demon changed the body too much or just outright killed it. But I had to try.

I grabbed everything I needed and headed back for the door. To my irritation, Sandy was already waiting next to my car. "What are you doing?" I asked.

"I'm coming with you."

"Like hell!"

"I'm your apprentice. I'm supposed to learn this stuff," she argued.

"You're my apprentice to learn exorcisms and dybbukim, not Christian monsters, that's a different class," I said, unlocking the car and getting in. She pulled open the door before I could relock it and got in too. "This is too dangerous, Sandy."

"I saw you getting exorcism gear too, that means whatever you plan on, you're supposed to teach me."

I glanced at the backpack in my lap, filled with gear I usually reserved for dybbukim. She wasn't wrong, which was infuriating. Why protect her from an angel and then feed her to a vampire?

"Okay, okay, but when we get there, you are going to stick with me, do what I say when I say it, and you're going to be extremely careful. I don't know much about these things; we're going in mostly blind."

"Okay ..." That sounded a little less sure. I realized that Sandy saw me as something of a superhero: I fought evil, I rescued her from a werewolf, I banished scary ghosts. Me not knowing much may be worrisome to her. "Okay," she repeated. "So, what do we know?"

"We know that there are a lot of different kinds of

creatures called vampires. So, the word itself is sort of useless; in this case, apparently what the Catholic Church calls a vampire is a demon."

"Like Sheydim?" Sandy asked, a little confused by the word. I didn't blame her.

"No, not like the Sheydim. That's the problem with religion and the supernatural, everything sort of gets lumped into binaries. Oh, this is an evil spirit with powers, must be a demon, or must be this or that. Oh, a woman did something you don't understand? Must be a witch!" I shook my head. "If you ever have the misfortune of seeing a Baptist exorcism, they are sure every ill thing in the world is caused by Satan and that Satan is possessing anyone who doesn't act the way they think they should."

"Wow, Christians are really obsessed with Satan, huh?" she mused.

"Yeah," I agreed, though I didn't want to mention how obsessed everyone was with the idea of the devil.

"But we don't believe in Satan," Sandy said slowly, probably looking for confirmation that Satan didn't exist.

"Well ..." I said, waffling a bit. "Here's the thing; we believe in Satan, but not in the way the Christians do. Satan isn't the devil."

"And we don't believe in the devil," Sandy pressed, wanting a more concrete answer.

"Eh, Jews tend to call it the Evil Inclination or blame Samael or Sheydim for the stuff the Christians blame on Satan. The truth is we all search for some external source of misery and evil. No one wants to be the cause, no one wants to take on responsibility. But that's all it is. Are there super powerful creatures that I would call evil? Absolutely, but none of them cause human cruelty, none of them are responsible for the things we do to one another. We don't share blame for that."

Sandy sat with that for a few minutes before nodding.

"So no, not Sheydim," I said, pulling the conversation back to the task at hand. "In this case, I call things that are outside of normal creation demons. They don't fit neatly into categorization, so I push them into the 'other' column. This thing, this vampire, according to Father Jerry, it's just one demon that can possess multiple people all at once. Since it's possessing people, that means maybe we can exorcise it. But it's more than a little dangerous."

Sandy's eyes grew wider as I described what we would be facing.

As we got out of the car, Sandy was pretty quiet. After the ride, the only thing she really knew about demonic vampires was how it was going to try to kill us. But maybe that was best. She needed to be afraid. Being an exorcist, let alone a hunter, didn't mean being fearless. Being afraid was the only thing that kept us alive. Unless it was something that could smell fear, then you should lock that down immediately. Could this vampire sense fear? It was possible; after all, at least according to the woman I had fought in the church, the creatures were insect-like. Probably able to sniff out pheromones.

Supposition aside, however the Catholics were tracking these things, I knew that this empty office space was the last known location. I was hoping that coming during the day would mean that it was asleep. But who knew how many of the stories told about vampires were true and how many were just the imagination of overzealous writers. Writers were the bane to any hunter. Stories, folk tales, rumors, all written as fact that led to too many dead hunters.

When we got to the doors, I pulled out a small set of lockpicking tools. I had started practicing the skill fairly recently. Over the last couple of years, I had to break into more things than I was really comfortable with. Kicking holes in glass doors was one thing, but the truth was that hunting down these creatures meant I needed to get into places where critters were hiding and trying to stay private pretty much anytime I left the house. Which meant trying to get through security systems. Luckily, most supernatural creatures, to my knowledge, didn't sign up for the hi-tech solutions. They opted for locked places that they could sneak into.

Well, now I would be able to sneak in too. In theory. I stood hunched over the lock for a few minutes, trying to unlock muscle memory as I pressed on the pressure pick and ran through the internal mechanisms of the lock, trying to get things to catch.

"Have you done this before?" Sandy asked.

"Of course I have." It wasn't a lie, I just hadn't done it on a standing door, to an actual office building, out in the open, knowing there was a literal blood sucking monster on the other side of the door. After several moments, the lock clicked and the pressure pick slid over as I unlocked the door. It was a rush; I felt like a super spy. I grinned wildly over my shoulder at my much-less-impressed-than-she-should-be apprentice. "See, nothing to it."

She rolled her eyes at me, but I didn't let that spoil my sense of triumph. I had just picked my first actual lock, and now I just needed to deal with a demonic mosquito monster. That was sobering. I dropped the smile and gestured for Sandy to stay quiet. We needed to get in, locate our target, and immobilize them. I pulled open the door and slipped inside the building, working hard to take careful, quiet steps. The last thing I wanted now was to give my position away and let my prey become my hunter.

Chapter 12

We had cleared at least four of the six floors, and I kept wondering if this was a smart move. After all, wouldn't I be more likely to run into a security guard than a vampire? It could also be a prank. Jerry had pulled small pranks before. It was his way of trying to keep this life light. Maybe after the heaviness of asking about a rogue prophet, he had felt the need to send me on a snipe chase. Of course, if it wasn't a prank, it was a deadly situation. I had my hand gun out, just in case.

I was about to call it, take us back down stairs—we could hit the boiler room or sub-basement, which felt more appropriate anyway—when Sandy grabbed my arm and pointed silently. She was a fast learner; keeping silent on a job like this was a matter of life or death. I followed her finger and gaze to a dark blotch on the hallway carpet. Well, that was a nasty stain. I moved over to it and dropped to one knee, touching the stain. It squelched under my fingers, still moist. The smell of iron stung my nose even before I brought my fingers up to look at the red liquid coating them. I knew it was blood. I glanced up and saw that the stain was actually a streak; someone had been bleeding profusely as they were dragged away. I glanced at Sandy; she looked pale, uncertain. I could always send her back out, tell her to wait in the car while I dealt with this.

But we were losing daylight, and I would need to escort her back down to the doors. Until we eliminated the threat of the vampire, I had to assume it was anywhere I wasn't presently looking. Instead, I waited until she met my eyes, then lifted an eyebrow and offered her a thumbs up. Not a great way to ask if she was okay, but it was all I had. We should probably learn sign language if I was going to do more excursions like this with other people. She looked at me like I was insane, but then fixed her eyes on the blood smear that left a trail through the hall to follow. I figured that was close enough to a let's-do-this as I was going to get.

I turned back to the stain and began following it, careful to walk outside of the mess. The last thing I needed was to leave a trail of bloody shoe prints for the cops to follow once they found this mess. I paused at the edge of a doorway; the streaks of blood went inside. If I was lucky, our quarry would be inside. I was hardly ever lucky.

I stepped forward and turned at the same time,

raising my gun to point into the room in case anything was about to leap out at me. Nothing. Well, not nothing. The mangled corpse of a security guard was laying in the center of the room. It was hardly recognizable as a human corpse, but the tattered, blood-stained uniform that was mixed in with the gristle and meat was a dead giveaway.

I peered into the corners of the room, looking for any sign of the creature on the floor. When I saw nothing, I stepped through the threshold and looked up. There it was.

I held up my free hand to signal to Sandy that she should not follow me. I pointed up and slowly stepped past the apparently sleeping creature so that I wasn't directly under it. I don't know what I had expected, maybe hanging upside down like a bat, or lying flat on its back against the ceiling like some sort of upside-down vampire from the movies. Three panels of the suspended ceiling had been removed, and the creature clung to the underside of the concrete partition, its six limbs gripping pipes and wires to keep it in place. All of the eyes I could see form my vantage spot were closed. I assumed it was dormant, not actually asleep—I don't know if demons actually sleep. I could have shot it in the head easily; maybe that would have killed it, though I doubted it. But I didn't want to kill them if I didn't have to.

I glanced at Sandy, shaking my head to warn her. She had pulled out a small 9mm hand gun. I didn't approve of giving kids guns. But ever since Stübbe had kidnapped her, I didn't feel like leaving anyone in my life unarmed. I knew Rivkah had been taking her to the range, I just hoped it wouldn't end in her shooting me. I gestured her in and guided her to maneuver around both the vampire and the dead body so she could watch my back. I gestured at my eyes and then pointed at the vampire, hoping she would take the hint not to take her eyes off the thing. She gasped in shock, seeing the creature there. I could tell she was trying not to shout at the sight of her first real monstrous being.

I was ready for violence, but I didn't want it to come to that, not if it didn't have to. I wished life could be as easy as TV shows made it out to be. Draw a circle in some holy oil and then the demon was trapped. But I didn't have any good magic circles, not for trapping demons anyway. I didn't even have any oil, holy or otherwise. All I had was a few spells, a few true words, and an exorcism ritual that seemed to work most the time. Of course, I had never tried it on a demon before, so this was going to be an entirely new experience in a lot of ways.

All I had was theories, and it was time to put them to the test. I reached into my inner pocket and pulled out a piece of chalk. With Sandy making sure the thing didn't move until I was ready, I knelt on the ground and began to draw. Draw is probably not the best word. I wrote the names of angels, prayers, and invocations in Hebrew in a circle around myself. I looked around, staring at the names. I dropped my backpack onto the ground and reached into it, pulling out a shofar and a small Sefer Tellihim—a pocket edition of the Book of Psalms. It was always better to be prepared. I finally pulled out a bit of incense shaped into a cone and set a lighter near it. I didn't want to light it until I was ready because the smell would surely wake the monster.

I silently asked G-d to order these angels to assist me, to be at my back and to carry forth my commands. I raised my hand, fingers splayed open, and took a deep breath and whispered. "çÈùÈÑä"

I spoke the command "be still," doing my best to speak it in the true pronunciation, and clenched my hand into a fist. The word roared from me despite my attempt to whisper it. Sandy dropped to her knees, shocked by the sudden sound, as reality itself writhed around the vampire, which was suddenly very awake. It's eyes, which covered its face and shoulders, flew open, staring at me with open malice. But it couldn't move, it couldn't scream at me, trapped in my command to be still and silent. Sandy stared in awe at the trapped creature, trembling a little. I understood; the first time hearing true pronunciations paired with looking into the eyes of the insect-like possessed man was a lot to take in. But I needed her to have a clear head.

I flipped open the small book and thumbed my way to the proper Psalms. I made a mental note to get a similar book for Sandy. Most Exorcism rituals combined notes from various apocryphal texts and writings with prayers pulled from the Book of Psalms. There were arguments within arguments about which psalm should be used in which situation. There were psalms of protection, of aggression, of healing and pleading for forgiveness.

For the possession of a human by a horrible blood sucking demonic force, which psalm would have the most meaning? I thumbed through the psalms and landed on Psalm 91. That would work as well as anything. I handed the book to Sandy.

"Read this, repeatedly, don't stop until I tell you to. Concentrate on thoughts of protection, on your safety, my safety, and the safety of the poor person that is possessed."

Sandy looked at me, wide eyed and freaked out, but nodded, taking the book from me. It still took her a moment to look away from the monster and at the book, but after a few seconds, her shaky voice began slowly going over the Hebrew. I wondered if the shakiness was an unfamiliarity with reading Hebrew letters or if it was from fear.

It didn't matter, she was reading, and hopefully, her mind was fixed on us not dying. I lit the incense and took several seconds to steady my mind, letting the soothing smell ease Sandy. I needed to stop procrastinating.

I took a deep breath and lifted the shofar to my lips, the feeling of the curved ram's horn was comforting, it was familiar. A blew out a shevarim, a blast of three medium length notes. Around us, the world fractured.

Not literally, but around us, in the room, the energies were shattered. Including my command to be still.

The possessed man fell from the ceiling, startled by the sudden absence of unseen bindings, and hit the floor with a heavy thud. I moved quickly, grabbing the possessed by the back of his neck, careful to avoid the eyes and little spines that I could see along his neck, and pushed down, hoping I would be strong enough to pin him down. I spoke quickly, angelic names, Hebrew prayers, all flowing together as I prayed over him.

He laughed.

Two of his arms bent the wrong way, reaching backwards to grab me, two hands on my shoulder, one on my neck. He was much stronger. His head turned 180 degrees to look back at me, the bones in the neck under my hand cracking and grinding together as they moved unnaturally. "Idiot fool. Your words have no power on me. I am not a servant of your G-d. I am no weak spirit or dybbuk for you to control."

He lifted me from the ground, his limbs moving at unnatural angles to push himself off the floor. He laughed again, his long mosquito like proboscis quivering as he laughed. His eyes, the primary eyes, where his human eyes would have been, were bulbous and compound, glowing red with some infernal light. I struggled against his hold on me. I could feel the eyes on his hands squirming against my skin.

"We can help you; we can remove the monster," I rasped, trying to get air into my lungs.

"The body, my little suit of meaty armor, is dead. The ruah trapped with me watching out as I enjoy the world through him. There is no leaving, there is no life without me." He laughed again, throwing his head back.

The world was swimming as he continued to choke me. Somewhere in the distance, I could hear Sandy's panicked prayers as she continued to read from Psalm 91.

"I'm going to tell you something," the demon chortled, bringing me close as he walked, effortlessly holding me off the floor.

I could feel the cold slimy flesh of his cheek as he pressed against me, one of his compound eyes brushing my skin. It made me nauseous.

"I'm going to throw you out of the window here. Then I will possess the girl. I'm going to take her, and I'm going to have her tell everyone how you abused her, how you used her for your own sexual satisfaction." He lowered his voice into a sinister whisper, as though sharing a juicy secret. "I won't change her, but I'll use her too. I'll enjoy drugs and men and all those things that break you humans so easily. Then I'll leave her rotting in a ditch. That is what I think of your angels, what I think of your G-d."

"One ... question," I rasped. "Can you do all that with a stake in your fucking heart?"

I jammed my hand up, driving the long, sharp piece of ash under his ribcage and up into his heart. While he was going on with his threats, I had pulled the weapon from my coat. Always have a backup plan.

The effect was instantaneous. He dropped me and staggered back, screaming. His body was coming apart as though he was made of ribbon paper being burned by an invisible flame. I had seen it before from the woman that Jerry had staked. But that had been right on top of me. Now I could see the way his body was disintegrating. His screams echoed in the empty office room as, bit by bit, he turned to ash. The whole process probably took less than a minute, but when you're standing there watching a man disintegrate, watching the pain as his body is unmade, it felt like much, much longer.

When the screaming stopped, I realized that Sandy was still chanting out the prayer; it was choked with sobs. It took me a moment to calibrate. I hadn't really been injured at all. Sandy had been threatened, though I didn't know if she even heard the threat, but she was unhurt too. I had hoped to save the possessed, but all in all, this was a good hunt, no one needed stitches. I waved at Sandy, trying to catch her attention, but her eyes were glued to the book as if she were trying to block out everything else.

I walked over to her and touched her shoulder. She leapt back with a scream, dropping the book, staring at me with huge round eyes. Seeing it was just me, she broke down and flung herself at me in a tight hug, crying into my chest. She hadn't been ready to see something that inhuman. I shouldn't have let her come.

I rubbed her back slowly, shushing her. "It's okay, it's okay," I promised her.

After a bit, she pulled away from me, wiping her nose on her sleeve. "I'm sorry, I, that scared me way worse than I thought it would. I thought it would be like with the dybbuk in my bathroom."

I shook my head. "No, it's okay to be freaked out, it's okay to be scared." Inside, I wondered if this was actually a good thing. If she was scared of monsters, maybe she would stop being interested in hunting the things and focus her attention on the way less deadly practice of just doing blessings and exorcisms. I could hope. At the moment, I was just grateful she hadn't pulled out her gun and shot me on accident.

"Let's get out of here," I said, kneeling down to replace all of my tools and gear in my bag.

With this out of the way, I needed to concentrate on Isingway's brother. I retrieved my stake from the pile of ashes in the middle of the room, watching them for a moment to make sure it didn't start to reform or something. When it didn't, I nodded and headed for the door, Sandy trailing after me.

Chapter 13

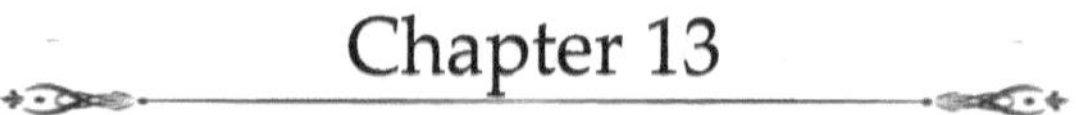

I dropped Sandy off up north with Rivkah, who looked askance at me. I didn't want to go into the ins and outs of what happened. I was sure Sandy would tell her all about it, and then tomorrow I would need to explain what *actually* happened. But for now, the two of them were safe and I could worry about the more dangerous part of my day.

I laughed to myself as I drove away. Only I could consider being choke slammed by a vampire to be the safer part of a day. But I had picked a fight with an inhuman assassin that knew where I lived and had already tried to kill me once. So, you know, perspective. I thought about trying to contact Isingway. I should tell him my plan, or at least some basic idea of my plan. Hell, maybe a Sheyd could help me take on a ghoul. But I didn't actually have a way to get in touch with the fae creature. So far, he had found me and contacted me every time. My mind flashed to the summoning ritual I had used when chasing Stübbe, but I didn't want to do that. There was only a small chance I would even contact the right being, and contacting the wrong thing would probably leave me fucked.

Instead, I would go get some dinner. I headed to the local pho shop and sat down to some noodles, considering all aspects of what I was doing. Almost everything going on in my life was bucking against the accepted and defined tenets of my faith. I shouldn't be teaching a child any mystical tradition; she needed her foundation firmly planted in Torah, Talmud, and Mishnah before even glimpsing behind the veil. But then again, I wasn't afforded that comfort either. According to minhag and halacha, tradition and Jewish law, I needed to be a married man, and then, and only then, would I be close to an age to begin a study of Kabbalah. Teaching a teenage girl barely past her bat mitzvah was strictly off limits.

Of course, the rules for the Beit Din were sometimes stretched and bent out of shape. The rules were written in another age and written mostly by men who had not taken the practical application of magic and mysticism into account. If we ignored Sandy, she would eventually be killed or driven to dire straits by the creatures that had become aware of her. If we didn't give her the tools to deal with them, then we were essentially condemning her to misery at best. That wasn't something I was okay with.

Nathan and I often bumped heads over our interpretation of Torah and the rules of engagement. But he knew as well as I did that we had to act in the moment and do whatever possible to protect and preserve Jewish life. I don't know how Nathan would feel about my current predicament. Dealing with Sheydim and ghouls. He wouldn't approve, and honestly, he shouldn't. All of this was happening because of choices I had made, so his sympathy would be as low as his condemnation would be high.

But the Sheydim were not evil. As much as the Talmud warned us to avoid them, they weren't by nature evil or unclean. They were just different. Souls that were half built, unfinished. They were immortal, but they were alive. Were their lives as sacred as a human's? I couldn't imagine why they wouldn't be. There was a story in the Talmud about Ashmandai helping a blind man because it would secure his place in the world to come. Why would a creature with no redeemable traits worry about that?

Isingway seemed nice enough too; though, of course, any of them could be play-acting. Luring me in to some terrible doom. It was a slippery slope, assuming that someone was out to get you; before you knew it, you were thinking that way about everyone. Paranoia is a common side effect of being aware of the supernatural. Maybe that's organic—knowing how much danger and how many dangerous creatures are out there keeps you aware that, at any time, they could come for you.

Or maybe it's not. Maybe it's a sentient force driving humans mad with fear, forcing them into insanity as a self-defense mechanism to keep humanity as a whole from learning about the supernatural world.

Now I was paranoid about some sentient maliciousness driving me insane. I was just a few steps away from putting on a G-ddamn sandwich board and screaming at pedestrians.

I finished my pho and got back in my car to head home. I had just pulled out of the parking lot when I realized that *he* was in the back seat, the glowing green cherry of his necrotic cigarettes giving him away in the shadows. It took a lot of willpower not to piss myself.

"You have balls, Wolf."

"I prefer if you didn't smoke in my car," I said in response, hoping that he didn't hear the quiver in my voice or see the way I was gripping the wheel tight enough to turn my knuckles white.

Whatever he saw or heard, he just chuckled.

"Big balls." He inhaled and blew a cloud of thick musty smoke into the front seats of the car. It was almost enough to obscure my vision. "You asked your little puppy to come find me. He came and found me, and I found you. Now why did this happen?"

"First, Shalnacht isn't my dog, he's yours. Or at least he's Baalrachius's. I recall him setting up that little ambush; it wasn't exactly a fun time for me. But yeah, I needed to get a hold of you. I think it's time we shared some information and maybe set some boundaries." I spoke with more confidence than I had. But it wasn't completely unfounded. I hadn't set these dominoes up without being prepared to watch them fall.

"I don't believe you are in a position to ask for anything, Wolf." He leaned forward and whispered in my ear. "Least of all, boundaries."

I lifted my hand from the steering wheel, reached into my coat, and withdrew a silver-dollar-sized coin, which I twirled between my fingers in front of his face. There was Hebrew on each side. One side read, *I am dust*; the other said, *The universe was made for me.* I couldn't see his reaction, but he hissed in a breath and I heard him sit back. He didn't know what the medallion did. I pushed a little bit of intention into the spinning coin as it moved between my fingers, making it glow a soft orange.

"I think I can ask for some personal space," I said, keeping my eyes on the road as I hit the highway.

"What do you want, Ze'ev? Why did you reach out to me?" he asked.

He used my actual name; he was taking me seriously. Just like I thought, he knew nothing about magic. Which made the gathering of spells an even bigger mystery. He was getting them for someone else. But who? Baalrachius famously despised magic users. Who else would Grin be serving?

"I have two questions, Grin. The first is why were there ghouls with Peter Stübbe when he broke into my study, hurt my assistant, and kidnapped my apprentice?"

Mr. Grin chuckled from the back, and I saw the cherry of his cigarette move as he shook his head. "I wouldn't know that, Ze'ev. Ghouls aren't some hive mind conglomerate that knows the thoughts of all of its parts. Maybe they had some personal stake in the matter, maybe they were mercenaries. Whatever they were, they were not following my directives in working with the werewolf."

I noticed he knew exactly who Stübbe was. The only thing he denied was having personal involvement in that. I didn't know if I believed him, but I had other things I needed to worry about immediately.

"I also want to know why you broke into my safe," I said, palming the coin and slipping it back in my coat. I had made my point.

He didn't answer immediately, taking another long drag of his cigarette. I reached over and opened the passenger side back window a crack, giving his thick necrotic smoke an exit that wasn't my lungs.

Finally, he answered. "We both know the dance we do, Ze'ev. You are tracking down the books because I ordered you to, but you have no intention of giving them to me. You hide them in your little safe while you think of a way to try to stop me from hurting your friends and your family. I, on the other hand, have to balance your usefulness against the trouble you cause. Something you may want to consider next time you send someone to find me."

At least the little game we were playing was full out on the table now.

"And why do you want them? You're no practitioner, neither is Baalrachius. So why the hell do you even want these texts?"

"How do you know I can't use them myself?" he asked.

I met his eyes in the rearview mirror, raising one of my eyebrows. "That's a weak-ass bluff, Mr. Grin."

He grunted his acknowledgment and shrugged. "There are members of the monstrous courts that may, not all are bereft of talent like me, allies."

"Allies for what, Grin, what is your goal?" I asked.

From the corner of my eye, I saw him toss his cigarette out the window. Everything was dark and quiet for a minute; the only sound was the wheels on the asphalt of the highway as I headed back towards my apartment. I thought he wasn't going to answer me. I wondered what would happen when I stopped the car. Would he just get out and walk away? Or would he decide it was finally time to deal with my troublesome ass?

When he spoke, it was quietly, so soft that I almost missed it over the thrum of the road under the wheels. "I'm going to kill Baalrachius. I am going to take his throne."

I was too stunned to respond at first. What could you say to a man-shaped monster who had just admitted to regicidal thoughts? Not just thoughts, but plans, actions. I didn't know enough about the politics of the monstrous world to know what such an act would do, but killing a creature who had held the ghouls in check for ten thousand years wouldn't lead to anything positive.

I drove the rest of the way in silence. I didn't want take him to my home, or to my workspace, though I knew he knew where they were. So instead, I drove to a closed outlet mall and stopped the car. Neither of us moved for a very long time.

Finally, I heard the back door open and Grin got out.

"Think about this carefully, Ze'ev. A war is coming, and as always, there will be a right side and a wrong side, there will be a winner and a loser. You think yourself Switzerland, innocent and neutral in the coming storm in the supernatural world. But you can't be. No one can be, not even the ignorant will be free from the effects of what comes, especially not the ignorant. If you think to stand against me, if you make yourself an enemy, it will be great pain that awaits you and yours. I would offer you this advice: choose your sides carefully. Because Baalrachius will not be careful with you or with humanity." He closed the door.

I watched him walking away, lighting another cigarette, in my side-view mirror until he was out of sight and then let out a long-held breath of air. That was not the answer I had expected, nor was it the one I would have hoped for. Things would be bad either way, honestly. I didn't know what his threat about Baalrachius meant. For at least a few thousand years,

Baalrachius had been careful enough, keeping his empire alive, his position solid, and his people out of sight of humanity. Then again, I didn't know how old Grin was or when he entered the picture.

He claimed to have allies too. What allies? By and large, or at least to my knowledge, the various supernatural communities of the world kept to themselves, watched after themselves. Of course, I had only recently heard of something called the Monstrous Court. I still didn't know what that was, and truthfully, until now, I had almost forgotten about it. Now it seemed more pressing. How could I find out more? It wasn't like I could just go google the ancient secrets of ghouls.

I mean I could. I had. But that wasn't actually useful; 99% of the shit you see on the internet regarding magic and unnatural creatures is conspiracy theories and the other 1% is propaganda. If there was some sort of organized force of monstrous entities, an inhuman illuminati, I doubted they would allow all their secrets to just exist on the cloud where anyone could find it. Despite the long-standing stereotypes of immortals being unable to cope with the changing times, most groups had at least one tech savvy individual in their number, or else they hired someone. Humans were apt to worship and follow anything that wasn't human; so long as it was in small enough numbers, it didn't upset the balance of things too much.

Was that the allies that Grin was talking about?

Someone like Basken? A chill ran down my spine and I had to shake it off. Obviously, Grin wouldn't team up with a necromancer like Basken; the entire reason I had gotten into Grin's crosshairs was because Baalrachius had been hunting the sorcerer. Ghouls hated the necromancers, and because I had levied the two groups against each other, the necromancer and his group had a healthy fear of the ghouls now. But still, the idea of some human trading favors with the ghouls for power, willing to use some of the most disgusting and vile ritualistic magic to do so, G-d knew what someone like that would be capable of.

I knew one person who could maybe help me find information, but it wouldn't be kind to ask him to look into it. But I didn't know if I had a choice. Better the devil you knew. I took one last look in the rearview, in the direction that Grin had disappeared, and started driving. I needed to stop his plan to overthrow Baalrachius. Hopefully, saving his decrepit hide would keep him from murdering me, maybe even make him forgive the sins I had committed against his people, both real and imagined. Now I just needed to figure out how to find and protect the King of Ghouls from his own assassin and some unknown occult practitioner.

Chapter 14

Keeping in mind that I had to have dinner with Sara's parents in less than twenty-four hours, I wanted to get as much done as I could now. I would visit Anthony, do some research, prep some talismans and spells, and then maybe set up some traps. Then I would make time to take a nap, groom, shower, and show up looking like a winner to sweep Sara off her feet and impress her parents.

That was the plan anyway. The reality of the situation was that I was largely anti-social and it was going to be awkward no matter how you cut it. But I couldn't worry about that now; there would be plenty of time to worry about meeting parents and not throwing away my relationship later. For now, I needed to worry about figuring out who Grin was teaming up with. What was the Monstrous Court that I had heard about? And where the fuck was Isingway?

I parked in the sketchy parking lot of Anthony's little apartment complex and headed up to his unit. I wasn't really worried about places like this; even in the bad areas, Austin was pretty tame. At worst, I would lose my wallet. But even that, I wasn't terribly worried about. I was a trained soldier with a weapon and a somewhat accomplished user of magic.

When I got up to the door, Anthony opened it before I knocked and stepped aside to invite me in. He had a disconcerting way of doing that, but that's why I was here, really. I remembered what Jerry had said over the phone. Did he already know about Anthony? Were they following me? The last thing I needed was to have the Catholic church gunning for me. I didn't think they would send some sort of assassins, but on the other hand, they weren't exactly known for their historic kindness or for respecting the sanctity of life. Was Anthony an honest to G-d prophet? It was widely accepted that the age of prophecy was over, and I doubted Anthony would feel like he was speaking to HaShem when he received his visions.

From what he described, the majority of his visions were nightmares, terrifying and obscure. Bits and pieces merged with symbolism that would haunt him for days or sometimes weeks after the event. He could induce the visions if he had to. Through meditation, mantras, and intense focus, he could access the ability to take glimpses into other realities, other times. The problem, beyond the psychological trauma of the experience, was that Anthony didn't have the knowledge or the experience to know what he was seeing.

He could be seeing a possible future or maybe glimpses into a realm populated by spirits. He could be seeing a possible future in a world populated by demons. Or, he could be seeing what some powerful Sheydim wanted him to see. That was also a possibility. There were creatures out there that could and would happily manipulate a troubled mortal to meet their own ends. That possibility was amplified by the fact that I didn't think Anthony was entirely human. When it came to supernatural creatures, especially the Sheydim, it was best to question everything.

"Hi, Ze'ev." Anthony's soft voice pulled me back to the present moment. "What's up?"

I decided not to tell him about my call from Jeremy; the last thing he needed to worry about was the Catholic church being interested in him. He might go looking, especially if he knew they thought he was a prophet. He was a Christian, and I was worried his blind faith in their institution would lead him into danger.

"I … need your help," I admitted. I didn't want to beat around the bush. I wanted him to know I was here to take advantage of his curse for my own use, again. "I'm a bit worried I may have bitten off more than I can chew."

Anthony nodded. He was stoic, though I could see him deflate a little bit; he wanted answers. Well, more than that, he wanted a cure. He wanted to be free of the curse of his visions, not be dragged into them more. I felt for him, I did, but I didn't have a lot of options.

"Yeah. You do that," he said flatly as he walked into his kitchenette area and grabbed two little mugs to pour tea he had been steeping before he answered the door.

I wondered if he had something like prophecy peripheral vision, something that allowed him to sort of know what was coming without the pain of full-fledged visions. Something to explore later.

"I do," I admitted, sitting on his futon couch, watching him as he set a mug of tea in front of me. "Specifically, I think I've gotten embroiled in a supernatural plot towards regicide. But without more information, I can't stop it, or even know if I should try to stop it. I think I should."

"Regicide?" Anthony asked.

"King-killing," I clarified.

"No, I know what the word means, I just ... who has kings? I mean, I've heard that there are monarchies in Africa and Asia ..."

"There are active monarchies all over the world, actually, they just tend to separate the head of the government from the head of state. However, most supernatural groups tend to gravitate towards monarchies. Powerful beings attain the title, they don't die, and just grow more and more powerful over time. The title doesn't change hands often." If at all. "But someone wants to force the issue and assume the throne."

"What group?" Anthony asked.

"Ghouls. The King of Ghouls is in danger, and I don't think that's a positive thing for humanity at the moment."

"Why?" Anthony asked, his bright green eyes the only indicator that he wasn't living with albinism.

This was the problem with adopting strays as students. I couldn't just tell him that I needed info, give him some money, and be on my way. He was allowed to ask questions. Asking questions was a cornerstone of my faith, or my culture. Even when I was in a hurry or busy, I couldn't brush off an honest question from someone I had promised to teach.

"Well, despite my personal issues with ghouls, they've coexisted on this planet with us for thousands of years at least. Baalrachius may be an evil old thing, but he isn't eager to wipe out humanity or make war or do anything insane like that."

"And you think his replacement would be?" Anthony asked, filling in the blanks.

"Well, they might be. Or they might not be. Or they may not be able to hold the proverbial throne. What I do know is that whenever the US gets involved and destabilizes a country, it never works out well for anyone. Not the country, not the previous government, and not the US. I think a power vacuum in the ghoulish ruling class would make for turbulent times; war touches everyone."

"But isn't you getting involved sort of like US

intervention?"

I grinned at Anthony. I didn't know if he was being a smartass or genuine, but he was a sweet kid. "Maybe, but they involved me first. I just need to know what I'm up against, I need to know who's pulling the strings on this one, because I don't believe I've got the whole picture here."

Anthony nodded, obviously unhappy that he needed to tap into his power, his curse, but willing to do it for me. I felt guilty about asking him to do it—desperate times, I told myself. He rose and walked to his tiny bathroom to splash water on his face. It was fascinating watching him pull himself into the zone to … do whatever it was he actually did. When I needed to dream walk or induce visions, I had to meditate, maybe use shrooms or DMT or some other hallucinogen to really get into the space where I could travel outside myself and attain a perfect perception of all the various aspects of the spiritual realm.

Anthony didn't do any of that. I think he would probably be completely freaked out if I suggested using drugs to him. He was so different than me. A good kid, charismatic, kind, with a pretty solid moral compass. It didn't feel great knowing that I could be a corrupting force in his life, not because I was trying to turn him towards being a druggie asshole but because I followed a code that was different than his and my world was far too dangerous to adhere to strict societal ideals.

Anthony sat down on his futon next to me and closed

his eyes. Taking several deep breaths, he reached over and touched my arm. I ignored my instinct to recoil; I wasn't a huge fan of touch. After a moment, his hand grew hot, uncomfortably so, and his grip tightened on my arm. His eyes were screwed up tight, but I could see a white light and mist pouring from behind the lids. His mouth moved in soundless chanting. After a moment, I could just hear him whispering.

I leaned forward to try to catch his words.

"The king is closer than you think, sitting on a rotting throne, pale hands grasping the reins of an empire that will not die. The serpents slither closer, their eyes on the king's throat. He doesn't know. He doesn't see. The moon is pale, a sliver of light climbing down his ladder into his well, into the submerged depths of hell. The crown falls. It is lifted, the hands … the hands …"

Anthony screamed, his eyes flying open. The light from his eyes burned bright, casting the room into sharp relief and angled shadows. He did not stop speaking.

"They came and then they came, one by one and in droves, they flooded the earth before the earth was flooded. With all of these eyes of heaven and hell, they watched and waited and wanted. These are those whose desires feast on the flesh of the first formed figures. Manipulating manipulators masticating man-made fate with teeth of iron and souls of fire. They came and then they came and they were sent and they will come and come again."

His grip was getting painful. His words were louder,

spat through clenched teeth. He was shaking.

I wasn't sure what I could do. He continued to speak, but the words weren't in English or in Hebrew. I caught some words that sounded close to Aramaic, or maybe even proto-Hebrew, but I couldn't decipher any of it. He continued for another 30 seconds, his words rising to a scream before he collapsed onto his side weeping.

I wrapped my arms around him, pulling him up and rocking him. I didn't know what he saw, but I could tell he was scared, terrified. He was still speaking, but now it was the babble of a boy who was scared out of his mind.

"Eyes, they're watching, always watching, and I don't think he can stop them, I don't think we can stop them." Tears streamed down his face.

He kept repeating himself over and over again, until at last, he noticed the cooling tea on the table and took a long drink. When he set the cup down, he looked at me and shook his head. The vision was already fading from his memory; he would see it again in nightmares. But he couldn't articulate what he now knew, not without too much effort. The only clues I could really take with me were what I could glean from his enigmatic muttered prophecy. I nodded.

After I made sure he was okay, I walked to the door. I still had to nap and get ready for my dinner with Sara's parents.

"Ze'ev?" Anthony called before I could close the door behind me.

"Yeah?" I asked.

"War is coming," he said softly, sadly.

"Yeah," I confirmed, though it wasn't a question. We both knew it was true, I just wish that I knew what it meant.

I drove to the office next. Luckily for me, Anthony lived on the south side of town like me. So going between his place, the office, and my house wasn't too much of a hardship. Once I was there, I checked the wards and traps, making sure that everything that should be in place was. Sometimes I felt like I was too paranoid, jumping at shadows and expecting Sheydim and monsters everywhere I looked. But history had shown me that, if anything, I wasn't paranoid enough! But I couldn't really ramp up my actions without alienating the world around me.

A lot of people who did the sort of work I did either died or turned in to hermits who lived in the woods shouting at trees to keep their distance. Neither proposition was very attractive to me. A handful got to retire, usually not hunters, usually only exorcists got to take it easy later in life. At least that's what I saw. But I wasn't just an exorcist. I was the thin line between the Jewish community and the supernatural world. A line that was getting thinner. No. That wasn't true. The line was where it always was. It was me who was getting worn down, frayed at the edges.

I pushed the door to my little converted office and

lab open and walked to my desk without bothering to turn on the lights. If this were a horror movie, I wouldn't have made it three steps before something emerged from the gloom and dark to rip into me. But this wasn't an episode of *Supernatural*. Domah wasn't going to step out of the shadows to inform me that I had broken some covenant and now I needed to set the next season up.

I had to deal with real problems, paperwork, relationships, safety. If I fucked up, it wasn't just that Sandy's or Rivkah's character got written out and then they went on to bigger and better roles. If we fucked up, we died. Painfully. And we would be forgotten, a footnote in a ledger on a shelf somewhere in New York. Filed by Nathan and left to gather dust.

I sat down at my desk and reached into one of the drawers to pull out a bottle of Milagro Reposado and a shot glass. I wasn't a big drinker, but I was tired and my nerves were shot. First by dealing with Grin, and then by Anthony's apocalyptic prophecy.

The moon being a sliver could mean anything. If it was actually a reference to the actual moon … well, the moon was waning right now, and it could mean that I only had days to stop Grin, or it could be next month, or in 5 years. But if Baalrachius was closer than I thought, did that mean he was back in Texas? Back in Austin? Why would he come here unless he wanted to make sure I was finally dead? Then there was the bit about descending his ladder into his well and a submerged hell. None of it made much sense. I sat back and stared off into space, trying to rack my brain with what it could possibly mean.

But his final prophecy kept spinning in my head. *"One by one and in droves, they flooded the earth before the earth was flooded."* His words seemed to point at Nephilim, the half angel, half human giants from the book of Enoch. Wicked creatures of myth that had been the cause for the flood, according to aggadah. In line with mythology, there had been three or four great wars against the Nephilim, ranging as far back to Abraham's day. Stories had been spun about magic swords and wars.

Og, one of the first Nephilim, had survived the flood by riding on the top of Noah's ark. But he had been killed centuries later by the Israelites fleeing Egypt. How many generations would such a creature be able to beget in that time frame? Where would they have hidden all this time?

I poured a shot and slammed it back. I was already pouring a second before I thought better of it. I stared at the full shot glass. This was the third path for people like me: drinking and drugs until sweet oblivion swallowed them and they found themselves on the streets living handout to handout. Slowly, deliberately, I put the bottle of liquor back in my desk.

There were giants; the Torah and the Talmud made it clear that the Nephilim were an ongoing problem. But they were mortal. David had killed one with nothing more than a stone and faith.

I could do it too. If Grin was working for, or with, Nephilim, they had to be stopped. I didn't have a sling, even my faith was a bit corroded, but it would have to do for now.

Chapter 15

I was in Crisp. It was the dream. I was sure of it. I couldn't remember the last time I had dreamed of Crisp or that day when I had stumbled across the horrifying truth of angels and monsters. But it used to be nightly. I used to suffer from insomnia because every time I would close my eyes, I would see this place. Relive that experience.

Of course, the events of that day, discovering Domah locked in mortal combat with something terrifying, something beyond any capable rational description, had led me to being the man I was. It had led me to training with Domah, learning magic and how to survive being a hunter. That didn't make it a happy memory, or a pleasant memory.

I looked down at my hands, my body. I was me, or rather, I was my adult self. Usually in these dreams, I was a child again, tripping along the dirt road between the house and the old barn. These dreams were always the same, never wavering from the path that would lead me to seeing that nightmarish thing again. It always felt fresh, as though I was experiencing the terror for the first time. I couldn't steel myself for it; even knowing it was a dream, even knowing that it was in the past and not real never seemed to lessen the tidal wave of fear that would wash over me.

I took a step and the city blurred past me, each footfall bringing me closer to the barn until I stood outside of the old barn where my life had changed forever. Maybe I was jaded by my experiences in the waking world, but I wasn't filled with the building dread of seeing the thing that would be behind the barn entangled with the bleeding angel; I just wanted to get it over with. I pulled the door of the barn open and stepped inside.

Nothing had changed, every surface was covered in grime and dust. The world inside the barn of my dream was frozen in time, incapable of changing its demeanor. It was completely separate from the waking world, in which I had actually spent days in this place studying Torah and Kabbalah. I felt like I was walking through syrup as I entered, like each step dragged. I didn't let that stop me; this dream was on rails that I knew too well. My feet seemed set to move of their own volition, carrying me further into the musty interior. I passed the desiccated corpse of a cow. It had died before I was born, and now it was just bones and leathery dead skin and sinew. Its head rose to watch me pass, but I ignored it. I knew it wasn't real, I knew this was just a dream. I could just jaunt past the cobwebs and dead cow and the desiccated man in the fine Italian suit on my way to the back door without any fear of being accosted.

I reached for the handle of the back door, the door that would lead me to where Domah would be entangled with the demon from beyond our reality, broken and bleeding but near victorious. Before I could grasp the handle, a sound like sandpaper being dragged across glass startled me. I whirled in place and faced the terrifyingly ancient man in the fine black suit.

His face was gray and dry, skin clinging to the skull like saran wrap. His eyes were milky and dead, but somehow, they pierced my soul. I didn't remember him. I had never met him; he was an intruder in a nightmare that was already unwelcome. His expression was one of anger, and it was terrible to see. I shrank back as he reached for me. In the distance, from beyond the door behind me, I heard the sound of loose chains rattling.

"Be not afraid. Fear is the enemy, the fuel, the power over adom." His voice was a discordant howl of intermingled voices. One deep, one a harpy's screech, and one a sibilant whisper. It echoed in my head. "I spoke, I warned, I asked. But still you press on, as is your kind's wont."

The sound of chains clinking and clanking was growing louder, distracting.

"Are you trying to stop me from opening the door?" I asked. It was a stupid question; I had opened this door decades ago, what was done was done.

"Yes, it is." The terrible old man answered my unspoken thought. "And now you must live with the consequences, you must act as you will act and know that none set the path before you other than yourself. Free will is the most wondrous gift, until you realize you have no one to blame but yourself!" He moved, so quickly I didn't have time to react, and grabbed my hand. I felt him press something warm and smooth into my fingers.

He pulled my hand, moving me. I couldn't resist. He turned me to face the doorway. To face nothingness. To face …

I woke up to the scream of my alarm clock. I lifted my hand to wipe the tears away from my face. I couldn't remember my nightmare, but it must have been a fucking doozy. I paused, realizing I was holding something. I opened my clenched fist and looked at the silver coin. It looked like a half dollar. One side was completely smooth, the other had the tree of life inscribed on it. It wasn't the normal ten-sephirot but the double length version. The one normally called Jacob's ladder.

It was named for the vision of the ladder that appeared before Jacob, who would later become Israel, as he fled into the wilderness. It prompted the statement that *G-d was in the place and I never knew it*. I turned the coin over in my hand, studying it for a moment. It reminded me of the other coin, the one I had used to fool Mr. Grin. I couldn't remember where I got that one, and I wasn't sure where I had found this one or why I was clutching it in my sleep. I didn't like coincidences. I rubbed my thumb across the engraved image of Jacob's ladder, my mind turning over the mystery of the coins. Too many mysteries in my life recently, the Ser'im with their kelipot, the Sheydim, Mr. Grin, and, of course, Anthony's prophecy.

If I could decipher any of these mysteries, I felt like the rest would fall into place. It was, in a way, similar to the sephirot of the Tree of Life. Each sephira was said to contain all ten sephirot, and within each of those were all ten again, into and from infinity. Only the Ein Sof, the infinite unknowable nothingness and the true nature of all things, including HaShem, was free from the refracting and reflecting nature of the sephirot.

That was one reason it was called a ladder. It was said that through climbing through the nature tree of life, you could ascend to heaven, like Jacob had seen. Or you could descend Jacob's ladder to the earth. Or his well. Jacob's Well. I gripped the coin with white knuckles as I rose from bed and paced. There was a watering hole not half an hour drive away called Jacob's Well. It was part of a massive submerged cave system. Anthony had said *"climbing down his ladder into his well, into the submerged depths of hell."* Jacob's ladder,

Jacob's Well.

Baalrachius was closer than I expected; was he there? At one of the most popular tourist spots in Central Texas, in plain sight? And if he were already there, how much time did I have before something terrible happened? Before Grin made his move?

I set the coin down on my dresser, next to the one I had found before, and moved into the bathroom. Whatever the time line was, I had to hope it could wait at least one more night. I had to go meet Sara's parents for dinner now. I showered and pulled on my pants before sitting down on the edge of my bed and staring down at my tallit katan.

The tallit katan was a small undershirt with fringes sewn into it. It was keeping with Talmudic law. I had a few of them; I wore one of them every day, almost without thinking about it, which, of course, was counter to the whole reason to wear them. To always keep the mitzvot in mind. But they, like my kippah, were simply part of my everyday dress, they were part of my identity. They sometimes brought grief when I had to deal with anti-Semites on a too regular basis, but they were me. Part of me, at least. Were they the part of me I wanted to present to Sara's parents? Were they a part of who I wanted to be in the future? Or were they a part of what was tying me to the dangerous and pain-filled life I was leading now? I ran my fingers through the fringes of the tallit katan, feeling frozen in indecision.

Sara wasn't religious and, as far as I knew, neither

were her parents. I knew distressingly little about her family. Maybe I was a shit boyfriend, having never really pried into it. Maybe neglecting my religious regalia would show Sara that I wanted to put her first, even above my obligations. But was that true? Was I ready to stay away not only from my duties as an exorcist but from the faith that had defined me all of my life? More importantly, did I need to set aside my faith in order to be happy and healthy? She had never asked me to, but it was clear that she just didn't see eye to eye with religious Judaism.

In the end, though, I had to present myself the only way I knew how. I slid the tallit katan over my head and stood to find a dress shirt to wear.

After a few more minutes of putzing around, I looked in the mirror. I looked Jewish; too Jewish? I had never worried about that before, why was I worrying about that now? I had always been unapologetically myself. My father, not Jewish himself, had always drilled it into my head to be proud of who I was and to never hide it. But now, on the precipice of meeting Sara's family, and hopefully salvaging my longest relationship to date, I doubted that, I doubted me.

Shaking my head, I left. I couldn't focus on that, I couldn't focus on myself. I left the apartment and popped in my car. I scrolled through my phone, through the last few text conversations I had had with Sara since we had our dinner. They were fairly straightforward. Me checking on her, trying to be affectionate without being clingy. Her answers were short and distant. It should have been an obvious sign, but we're all blind to signs when we've convinced ourselves otherwise. It was as true for the divine as it was for people. I was choosing to ignore those signs and convinced myself that I could save us.

Finally, I found the address where I was going to meet them, and, of course, it was farther than I had planned. The Salt Lick in Driftwood. It was always annoying how every visitor to the city always demanded to get barbecue.

I put the car in drive and headed out towards Highway 71. Maybe after dinner, I could continue down the highway from Driftwood and hit Wimberly, check out Jacob's Well after all. I would already be halfway there. That was assuming Sara's parents didn't want to get drinks or go somewhere else. I was trying to ignore the lump of lead in my chest and pretend everything was going to be okay.

After the thirty-minute slog down the highway to Driftwood, I pulled into the parking lot and started looking for Sara's car. I couldn't find it, but I supposed her parents could have picked her up. I rolled through the parking lot for a few minutes, considering where to park, completely oblivious to the fact I was avoiding parking and going in. I had convinced myself I wasn't afraid, that I wasn't at war with myself and my faith. I was about to slide into a spot when I spotted something that nearly made me piss myself.

There, at the entrance to the parking lot, was a gangly, misshapen silhouette. While I couldn't make it out entirely, I could tell that its frail limbs bent in the wrong ways in too many places. But worse than that, it clutched something in its hand. It seemed to emanate squalid darkness even in the low light of twilight. The sight of the dark glob it held twisted my stomach and hurt my brain. I knew what it was even from where I was. One of the kelipot that the Ser'im had carried, a shard of corrupted reality that drank sin.

They had said that they would stalk me, that they would hunt and kill me. But this was my first time seeing one of them since the zoo. I didn't need to wonder what it was doing here; it was after me. After me if I was lucky, anyway. Most supernatural creatures steered clear of public displays of violence. They wanted no part in exposing themselves or their kind to humanity. The Ser'im were obviously cut from a different cloth. Their first act had been to kill a bunch of wolves in a public place and wait in full site of the zoo staff for me to come to them. They weren't worried about exposure, they weren't scared to start shit or hurt the innocent.

I looked over at the restaurant. If I ignored the Ser'im there and went inside, maybe it would attack me or maybe it wouldn't. But it would certainly see me with Sara and her family. At the zoo, the things had killed an entire pack of wolves, not just one but the whole family. They would come for my family too. And my family's family. Going into the restaurant would be setting Sara and her parents up for being torn apart the same way those wolves had been. For fun.

I growled and turned my car to drive after the demon. I needed to take care of this, hopefully with enough time to get back and meet Sara for dinner.

Chapter 16

I gunned it towards the exit and the glob of darkness that marked the demon's presence. As soon as my headlights fell on it, it was off. The spindly hog-hyena-demon thing slipped into the trees and raced away. I hit the exit hard and fast, peeling out of the parking lot and back onto the highway, giving chase as best as I could. I could just make out the moving shadow and rustle of branches in the undergrowth beside the road to follow.

I could hardly keep the fast-moving creature in sight, using my peripheral to watch for oncoming traffic and to make sure I wasn't about to swerve off the road. Wouldn't that be a son of a bitch? Trying to stop a monster to save myself and then killing myself in a car accident? It would be on brand, as it wouldn't be the first time I was in a car accident while trying to stop some horrible monster. I smiled grimly as I pushed my senses to the limit to track the monster and follow the road. I wasn't sure where it was leading me or if it would even stop. But I was damned and determined to catch it, and face it.

As I drove, I did a mental inventory of what I had on me at the moment to deal with a demon. I had no idea what would actually harm it. But I was armed. I had my Jericho, a reliable and comfortable .45, in my glove compartment. I had a sanctified bat in the trunk, carved with the names of angels and warding spells—it was one of my deadliest weapons. I had my butterfly knife in my inner coat pocket—it wasn't magical at all, but it was sharp and I was pretty decent with it. Other than that, I had a simple protection talisman and my knowledge of magic to back me up. I was not confident.

I wasn't sure how long I chased the creature. At the time, my entire focus was on neither crashing nor losing sight of the bouncing ball of darkness leading me away from the Salt Lick and Driftwood like some sort of reverse Will-O-Wisp. It wanted me to chase it. It was leading me, I knew it, and I was sure it knew that I was aware of that. If it wanted to, it could just turn right and head off in a perpendicular route away from the highway and I would have no way to follow it. The fact that the Ser'im was staying where I could follow it was certainly proof that this particular game of cat and mouse was coming to a close.

Finally, it peeled off and away from the highway. I

took the exit, gritting my teeth in annoyance—it could at least pretend it wasn't leading me to my death. I could imagine it lazily running at top speed, a snide smirk plastered across its horrendous muzzle. It knew. It knew that I knew it was a trap. And it knew I didn't have a fucking choice.

Intrusive thoughts would only hinder me at this point, muddy my ability to fight and my ability to use the true pronunciations. I would need every tool at my disposal; I needed to be confident. When I had seen the demons before, it had freaked me out. I had been caught unaware by the appearance and demeanor of the Ser'im. Now I knew what was coming, I knew what to expect, and I knew that I was being lured not to my doom but to theirs.

I was building myself up. I had almost convinced myself of the veracity of my thoughts when I realized I was pulling into the parking lot for Jacob's Well.

I looked around the parking lot, trying to find that blot of darkness that would give the kelipot and its Ser'im owner away. At least now I knew what it was trying to do; it wanted to trick me into a confrontation with Baalrachius. But that actually worked in my favor. Maybe I could deal with everything all at once and be done with Mr. Grin and the Ser'im tonight. I had to be confident, I had to be sure of myself. I stopped the car and slid out after grabbing the gun from the glove compartment. I decided not to grab the bat; the bat was a nuclear option. With it, I could push my body past the limits of mortality, invoke the angels of strength and battle. An edge, sure, but it would also be very clear that it was the weapon that killed the ghouls with Stübbe; and if I wanted a chance to parlay with Baalrachius, I couldn't come bearing a missile. My knife, gun, and magic would have to be enough.

I looked around for security. I had only been here a handful of times, but I had to imagine such a hot spot, and one where teenagers loved to come, would have round-the-clock security. But I couldn't see anyone or anything moving in the darkness. It was possible they were just somewhere else in the park, but it was just as possible they were paid off or killed off by the supernatural threats present here. I needed to be careful. Another hardship of the job: I always needed to be careful about exposing my activities to humans. Unlike the Sheydim or Ser'im, I couldn't turn invisible or intangible and hide from my fuck-ups.

I waited a few moments for my eyes to adjust to the darkness and then headed down the path towards the spring. It had been so long since I had been here that I wasn't really sure what to expect. I knew that due to environmental concerns, there were several conservation projects going on with the well and the area around it. Fifty acres all told, though what that would do for water conservation, I did not know.

I kept my senses alive, trying not to focus on sight too much, allowing my mind to flow over the sounds, smells, and feelings in the air. I didn't know what the Ser'im's plan was. It could attack me in the middle of the path, having lured me to a secluded spot. Or, as I suspected, it could wait until a ghoul stumbled on me and did its dirty work for it. I clicked the safety off with my thumb as I walked, my gut instinct telling me that when shit happened, it would happen faster than conscious thought.

I was right.

The mass of muscle and loose skin hit me. The only warning I had was the smell of musty decay that preceded it by fractions of a second. I was knocked off the path and into the tangle of thorns and tall grass to the side of the gravel. Rising, I brought my gun to bear … on nothing. Hit and run. I climbed back onto the path only to be hit again from the opposite direction. It sent me tumbling off the path again, but this time it didn't disappear. It stood over me on thin, emaciated legs, it's disgorged belly and loose skin flaps dangling against me as it cackled and giggled. In one long-fingered hand, it raised the kelipot in all of its terrible glory above its head, glowing like the sun during a solar eclipse, a spot of pure blackness that seemed to emanate all the same.

With its other hand—a small gnarled thing that was so at odds with the elongated nature of its limbs— it struck at me, clubbing me with the malformed appendage. Each time it struck home, the nails of its crooked fingers dug in, causing me to bleed. I brought my arm up, trying to catch its arm under the elbow so it couldn't swing its fist at me, but the elbow just bent the other direction and it continued to flail. I brought my legs up, trying to work them between us while avoiding and blocking its strikes. The entire time it wrestled with me, its high-pitched, discordant squealing laughter echoed through the park.

I finally got my legs under the Ser'im and kicked it off me. I scrambled to my feet and faced the thing as it rose. It growled, its muzzle peeling back from the skull to reveal multiple mandibles ripping from the sides of its horrific mouth, a mouth filled with sharp, rotting teeth. I wondered if it was made this way or if it became. I didn't care to ask. I raised my gun and fired three shots. The first two struck the Ser'im in its center mass, driving it back; the third struck it in the head. An explosion of bone, flesh, and brains flew into the air, only to dissolve into smoke before they hit the ground.

The Ser'im staggered, not falling but not approaching. Its pus-coated eyes seemed to dart around, trying to find me, its jaw hanging open in shock and confusion. I hadn't thought a gun would be enough. But maybe it was, maybe I could end this threat with mundane means. I wondered about the dissolving flesh; was that just something that happened to demons? Like the vampire turning to ash before, perhaps the Ser'im and other demons couldn't hold themselves together, stay rooted in this reality, without conscious effort.

Separating the Ser'im's flesh from its form disconnected it from the willpower holding it together.

Despite humanity's obsession with and war against demons, which was almost older than human civilization itself, we knew so little, or what was known was closely guarded secrets by demon hunters. I had heard of demon hunters, of course. A small zealot cult with operatives who would whisk in and kill off demons and then disappear again, they were the cryptids of the hunter and exorcist world. Most of us didn't believe they were real. I tended to agree—after all, if they were real, then wouldn't they be here dealing with this fucking nightmare?

I walked forward. I would kick the creature into the water and fill it with enough holes to let the whole mess evaporate. One down, two to go. I lifted my leg and lashed out. Even as I kicked out, the Ser'im's eyes focused on me, its horrible maw twisting into a smile as it raised its kelipot. The sickening thing drank in the light, the darkness expanding as the demon grabbed my leg and twisted, hurling me through the air. I landed in the waters of Jacob's Well. I floundered a moment, trying to both tread water and not lose my gun; but swimming in dress clothes with a gun in hand and nice shoes on wasn't easy.

The orb of darkness, it had grown in size, emanating so much filthy black light that it actually obscured the Ser'im.

"Too easy." I heard the discordant squeal mocking

me from somewhere behind the light. "Too easy, not considerate, but I will win, I will win and my siblings will laugh as you scream."

I thought it was being a little premature. While I was certainly inconvenienced by being in the water, I wasn't out of the fight yet. I started swimming for the far edge, away from where the creature stood, when I felt something grab onto my ankle. I turned, trying to see if somehow the swine-hyena thing had jumped into the water, but it still stood there. I had just enough time to glance down and see the pale clawed fingers of the ghoul on my leg before it pulled me under, dragging me through the water.

Chapter 17

This was getting too familiar. I pointed my gun down and fired. It went off. I could feel the kick, I could hear the muffled *bumf,* but I couldn't see shit with all the water rushing past me as we torpedoed through the water. Who knew ghouls could swim so fast? I tried to calm myself, but I had no air, I had no bearing. I aimed down between my legs and fired again. This time my downward trajectory was finally stopped. Red filled the water around me. I was about to start swimming up when I felt the grip on my leg again, and once again, I was moving.

My lungs were burning as I was denied oxygen for far too long. I did everything I could to stop myself from gasping, but I had no air in my lungs. My body's autonomic responses were too hard to overcome, and I opened my mouth, taking in the fresh water in a gulp that set my entire body on fire in pain. I was going to die here and now. I couldn't fight water. I couldn't summon oxygen. I couldn't pronounce any magic words or bluff my way into gills. The world was growing dark.

Almost as quickly as it began, it ended.

I was thrown out of the water. I landed on a cave floor in complete blackness. I rolled onto my stomach and retched, coughing and trying to expel as much of the water as I possibly could. Everything ached. My lungs were on fire as I coughed and hacked up mouthfuls of liquid, but my entire body felt like it had been clenched far too tightly. But as quickly as I could, I pushed myself up and swung around, trying to get some sort of bearing in the utter blackness of the cave.

Suddenly, a light flared. Torches burst to life on the walls, and I realized I was in some sort of twisted cavernous cathedral. A church with pews and a throne on an altar all carved from the stone of the caves.

On the throne, dressed in an immaculate white suit, wearing a thin crown of tarnished silver, sat Baalrachius, the King of the Ghouls.

I turned slowly, taking in the surroundings. There were ghouls perched on every outcropping of stone. They all stared at me hungrily. Beside me, the ghoul I had shot had been pulled from the water and placed like a piece of guilty evidence. I ignored it, trying my best to look undisturbed, unafraid. I wasn't sure how I should behave. What was my move?

Slowly, I bent down on one knee and inclined my head towards the king. He may have been a monster, but he was also an earthly king, and maybe I could appeal to his sense of pride.

"I thought we killed you off. I was sure, in fact, that I ordered your death." His voice was a sibilant, the sort of voice you imagine whispered from a serpent offering an apple. "So, tell me, little Jew, how it is you come to be standing whole and breathing in my sanctum?"

I raised my eyes to the formidable visage of a creature that was thousands of years old and cleared my throat. "You did, you had, mighty king, but I fought my way free of your executioners, eluded your assassin, and in the end, led your subjects to the true antagonist you wanted dead." I decided to leave off the part about the demon tossing me into Jacob's Well; he probably knew about that already.

"You presume to know my thoughts better than I do?"

"Who needs to presume? You yourself said that you were hunting the necromancer." I paused, taking a breath, the fact that I wasn't dead yet a cold comfort at the moment. "But I am alive because you were betrayed, King." Time to toss my chips on the table, choose a side and end this thing once and for all. I could feel every set of ghoulish eyes on me, waiting for an explanation.

"Betrayed? This is an intense accusation, one I would need to hear more of. You have bought yourself another minute of life. Explain."

I rose to my feet. I could almost feel the tension of the ghouls around me as they tensed, ready to pounce, ready to kill. In the back of my mind, I considered what defense I could throw up to save myself. "Of course, your assassin, you sent him with orders to kill me. But I'm here, I'm alive, as you pointed out."

Baalrachius nodded, his long too-many-jointed fingers drummed on his chin. "Yes. I see where you are going with this. Yustef, come!"

I didn't know who Yustef was at first, but a moment later, Mr. Grin stepped out of the shadows. I could see the hate in his eyes as he stared me down. It was so odd, seeing these two, Grin in his black suit and tie, Baalrachius in his white suit, like day and night. All of the other ghouls were naked or wore rags and scraps.

Baalrachius didn't take his eyes off of me but raised a hand to gesture at me.

"Explain," he commanded.

Mr. Grin, Yustef, wasn't caught entirely off guard apparently. He raised his hands. "He is a wily little magician, my king." Grin stepped forward and smiled cruelly at me. "He is a trickster who aimed us at his enemies and then threw a shield up to protect himself from my wrath. He is not dead simply because I have been seeking a way to punish him."

"No, you found me, Grin," I interrupted. I could see where this was going. In a heartbeat, Grin would turn the congregation of ghouls on me and I would be ripped to shreds. "You found me and informed me that you could kill me at any time if I didn't gather books for you."

Grin began to laugh. "And why would I do that? Why would I ask you to gather spell books? I am no magician, no sorcerer. I do not hide behind magic to tear my prey apart!"

Baalrachius turned slowly towards Grin, his deep-set milky eyes glinting with horrible intent. "The mortal didn't say they were spell books, Yustef."

Grin paused, his smiled faltering and then falling away entirely. "My king—"

Was all he was able to get out before Baalrachius was on him, grabbing him by the neck and flinging him straight up into the air. There was a painful sounding wet slap as Grin collided with the roof of the cave.

"What I do not understand," Baalrachius said as he effortlessly caught the falling body by his shoulder and kept him suspended off the ground, "is why you would gather spell books. That is no lie that you cannot use magic, I can't smell it on you. What is your plan? Why betray me?"

Grin scratched at Baalrachius's arm, growling and whining like a feral dog caught in a cage. "You will fall. You have had your time, King!" the assassin spat.

All around me, ghouls were shrieking and gibbering.

"And you will end me? With what, Yustef? With what power?" Baalrachius raised his free clawed hand.

"With mine!" The voice cut through the din of the ghouls. It commanded silence. All present were shocked by the suddenness and the power it held. But no one, not one entity in that cave was more taken back than I was as Sara emerged from seemingly nothing and caught Baalrachius's claw in her hand.

I couldn't speak as I watched her causally toss the ghoul king aside. She was dressed in what appeared to be a running outfit, sports bra, sweat pants, nothing fancy, definitely not the sort of outfit she would have worn to dinner. She raised a fist—it was coated in a dark red that looked like blood—and gestured with her other hand. A wave of nausea spread through me as she used disgusting blood magic to pin Baalrachius to the floor. I watched Grin shake off his hurt and stand next to my girlfriend, a sly smile playing across his face.

"Go ahead … Yusie, play with him," Sara encouraged, her voice playful and full of sexual teasing as she turned away from them and faced me. She walked forward, her bloody fist still raised high.

Behind her, Grin drew a straight razor and approached the fallen king; and all around us, the ghouls were breaking into chaos and infighting, each choosing sides in a civil war that I had done nothing but speed up the time table for. But I was powerless to do anything at all. My eyes were locked on the woman I loved.

"Oh, Ze'ev … here we are … finally, really. It's been a long time coming." She paused and licked her bloody fist, her tongue—too long to be human, I realized— flicking sensually over the bloody digits. "I don't think it's going to work out, sweetheart."

"No, this is a trick, you're not Sara," I finally managed

to croak.

"Oh, but I am. I am … was, your girlfriend, for years. For years, Ze'ev, I put up with you, a disgusting excuse for a little pious man, going about your hypocritical path and fighting things that humans are just too stupid to understand. But you know what my favorite part was?"

I couldn't even bring myself to answer her.

"The lies. Ze'ev. The lies upon lies upon lies. Watching you squirm and spout deceit at every little opportunity. And do you know what I did? Every time you stood me up with some little lie about helping children or teaching a class? I would head to a bar somewhere, and I would fuck every man and woman in that bar until I drained them. I would drink their cum and bathe in their juices. And it was good. I looked forward to your lies."

My mind reeled at the enormity of what I was hearing, not just the joy she took in infidelity but the laughing knowledge that at every moment I had been the fool.

"But—" I started.

But she interrupted.

"The best lays, the best lovers, were those I rode as I pointed them at your throat, Ze'ev. Basken. Stübbe. Mmm, especially Stübbe." She rubbed her bloody hand over her body as though she were about to pleasure herself right then and there. "He was a beast, and he would whisper promises about how he would kill you while we fucked. I came hard with him."

She stopped right in front of me. I had my gun, I had my knife, but I couldn't bring myself to bring either to bear against her. I felt like I had a hole in my chest where all my willpower and hope were draining out, drip by drip. I couldn't feel at all, as though I was already dead. Sara. Sara was the "she" that had orchestrated so much of my pain. She had nearly killed Rivkah and Sandy … and me. All those kids, everything. What was she? What was this monster I had lain with, I had bared my soul to?

She raised her hand to strike me down. I closed my eyes and raised my head.

But the attack never landed.

There was a sudden rush of air as something pushed past me, and I heard Sara let out an enraged scream. Opening my eyes, I saw the towering form of some horrific demonesque praying mantis. It was long and drawn out, stretched too thin, but no part of it looked frail. Its chitin was black and red, with thorny growths. Whisp-like tendrils rose from its body, wrapping around and crushing any ghoul that got too close.

"Where is my brother, Pinza!" the creature, Isingway I now realized, roared as it swung its claws at Sara.

Sara, for her part, danced away from the swinging claws with a cruel laugh. "Is it not obvious, Sheyd? But don't worry your little head. He was delicious."

Isingway roared and pressed his attack. Taking advantage of Sara's distraction and of the chaos going on all around me, I rose and charged past the fighting. Grin was still standing over Baalrachius, blood dripping from the razor in his hand. Was I too late? I slipped my hand into my pocket and wrapped my fingers through the handle of my engraved brass knuckles. As I crashed into Grin, I rocketed a punch directly into the side of his head.

He had been so focused on Baalrachius that he didn't see me coming, and my punch landed with a very satisfying crunch as his jaw snapped like tinder and the side of his face caved. He flew aside and landed in a heap, but I knew that wouldn't be enough to kill him. Given the chance, he would heal, rise, and kill me. I glanced over at where Isingway was trying to murder my ex-girlfriend. Sara seemed to not only be holding her own but gaining the upper hand.

Forced with the decision to kill Grin or escape while I had an opportunity, I decided on self-preservation. Killing Grin would give Sara time to win and then murder me, murder Baalrachius, revive Grin, and it would be like I had done fucking nothing. I stooped and pulled Baalrachius's slender form into a fireman's carry and then ran as fast as I could carrying his weight towards the water. With a dive, I began kicking my legs. I didn't know where I was going, I didn't know these cave systems or which way freedom was. But I had to try.

I was running out of air when Baalrachius moved, coming out of his spellbound impotence. His long hand grabbed me, and he kicked. The water rushed past me as Baalrachius— a much stronger swimmer than I, apparently—pulled me along with him. Moments later, I was once again tossed onto the edge of the waters of Jacob's Well.

Gasping for breath, I unsteadily rose to my feet and looked around. I had lost my gun somewhere in those caves, but I would at least face the Ser'im or any other monster head on.

Nothing came.

I turned to look at the waterlogged King of Ghouls, who stood on the edge of the water looking down. I limped to his side and stared down with him in silence. I don't know how long we stood there like that, but eventually, Baalrachius shook his head and turned towards me.

"You saved my life, twice, I suppose. Though from the same threat. Why?"

I shrugged a little. "You've been king a long time, long enough to understand the balance, the delicate nature of keeping everything running. I don't trust ..." I gestured to the water, "them, to keep the peace."

Baalrachius nodded, accepting my words at face value. "There will be no peace, not for my people anyway. But I will do what I can to keep this war from spilling over into your world. Consider that my repayment of the debt." He turned and began walking away from the pool.

"What will you do?" I asked.

He paused and looked up at the moon above us. "I will find my allies, I will out my betrayers, and I will secure my kingdom. Despite what Yustef might think, this is not the first attempt at a coup, it will not be the last, though I am disturbed by the lilit'im's presence. It seems there are moves in the world of the Sheydim as well. All things will find their place in this, little Jew, yourself included." With those words, he continued walking, disappearing into the murk of night.

Chapter 18

It took me a little while to drag myself to my car; my leg didn't want to respond, my muscles were exhausted, unresponsive. When I got to my car, I saw Isingway there in the form I knew him in, a dapper looking gentleman. But he was torn up, beaten and bruised. I shook my head as I stepped past him to unlock the door. I didn't get in, though.

"I'm sorry," I said, not looking at him. "About your brother."

"So am I," he said. I could tell he had a lot to say but didn't know how to.

"Thank you," I finally said. "For saving me, for stopping her from killing me."

"Yeah," he said. I heard him move closer. "I couldn't kill her or the ghoul. I couldn't avenge Oro."

I turned to look at him. He looked like he wanted me to offer my help, to join his crusade against Sara and Grin. But I didn't say anything; I avoided eye contact. I had located the brother. I had found out what happened to him. That's what I had owed him, that's all I had owed him. I felt guilty for that, for thinking of myself, for being so selfish. But this was all over my head. It was too much.

Finally, I looked up and offered him my hand.

He was silent and unmoving at first. I was worried he would make it a demand, but instead, he just nodded and shook my hand before fading away into thin air. I stood there for a minute, maybe to make sure he was actually gone and not just invisible, before getting in my car and driving home. I considered calling Rivkah, or Nathan. Someone needed to know what was happening. Instead, I called my mom.

"Hi, Mom," I said, trying to put some steel in my voice, trying to speak past the lump of grief and heartbreak that had settled in my chest once the adrenaline had died down.

"Ze'ev? What time is it?" Her voice was a blessing; it soothed my soul the way only a parent could.

That thought made me miss Dad. My heart felt like it was being ripped apart with every passing moment. It was like when Lillit had held me in that moment of death for what felt like eternity.

"I'm sorry, Mom, I just …"

"Honey, what's wrong?"

"Uh, well … Sara and I broke up."

There was silence on the other end of the phone. I

realized it had to be extremely early in the morning for her in New York.

"Oh, honey … what happened?"

I couldn't tell her. All I could do was lie because I couldn't tell her the truth about everything. Even with her having a clue about what I did, she couldn't be exposed to the full terrible weight of everything that had gone down. But I couldn't lie either. I just didn't have it in me to lie anymore.

"I'm sorry, Mom, I wasn't looking at the time. I … I'm going to book a ticket and come visit, okay? I'll tell you what happened then."

"All right, honey. Well … text me the details when you get everything squared away."

"Okay, Mom. I love you."

"Love you."

I hung up and drove in silence all the way home.

Once home, I drew a bath and stared at my phone. There was nothing on it, no threats from Grin or promises of revenge from Sara. Nothing from Rivkah, Sandy, or Anthony. Sitting in the hot bath, I tried to rehash everything, I tried to put everything in perspective. But my brain refused to reconcile what my life was, what my life had become. I had been with Sara for a long time, years and years. And every minute of that had been a lie. Both from me and from her. I had loved her, but she had never cared about me other than to somehow use me in a plot to do something terrible.

And then she had tried to have me killed. And all of this because of who I was, because when I was a kid, I had been possessed by a dybbuk. Something from over twenty years ago was making my life hell now, and I didn't know how to make it stop.

Or did I?

I flicked my thumb across the screen, bringing up my text messages. I clicked on Nathan's name. He would be asleep; he was in New York like my mom. But he was also my boss, my connection to the Beit Din. I tapped my phone against my head, willing my brain to function, but it was all gray and a swirling mess of unclear thoughts. Finally, I typed my message and hit send. Just two words.

"I quit."

About the Author

John Baltisberger is an author of speculative and genre fiction that often focuses on Jewish Elements. Through his writing, he has explored themes of mysticism, faith, sin, and personal responsibility.

Though mostly known for his bizarre blend of Jewish mysticism and splatter, John defies being labeled under any one genre. His work has spanned extreme horror, urban fantasy, science fiction, cosmic horror, epic verse, and he has even written a guide for mindful meditation.

Beyond his writing career, John is the Publishing Editor of Madness Heart Press, a press focused on transgressive and experimental horror. He also runs the Jewish Speculative Fiction press Aggadah Try It, and the game company Madness Heart Games, where he works as the Creative Director. He lives in Austin, TX with his wife and his daughter.

You can see his work and more at www.KaijuPoet.com

More Books from

Aggadah Cry Jt

Treif Magic by John Baltisberger
isbn: 978-1-7348937-0-0

Son of the Right Hand by John Baltisberger
isbn: 978-1-955745-04-8

Giant Robots of Babael by Max Bauman
isbn: 978-1-955745-07-9

Scapegoated by Jeff Oliver
isbn: 978-1-955745-14-7

Of the Book: An Anthology of Jewish Horror
isbn: 978-1708473730

The Green Children Help Out by Gillian Polack
isbn: 978-1-955745-03-1